A ROBERTSON FAMILY CHRISTMAS

A ROBERTSON FAMILY CHRISTMAS

a novella

Tyndale House Publishers, Inc., Carol Stream, Illinois

MISS KAY ROBERTSON

with TRAVIS THRASHER

Visit Tyndale online at www.tyndale.com.

Visit the Duck Commander website at www.duckcommander.com.

Visit Travis Thrasher's website at www.travisthrasher.com.

TYNDALE and Tyndale's quill logo are registered trademarks of Tyndale House Publishers, Inc.

Duck Commander is a registered trademark of Duck Commander, Inc.

A Robertson Family Christmas

Designed by Dean H. Renninger

All Scripture quotations, unless otherwise indicated, are taken from the Holy Bible, *New International Version*,® NIV.® Copyright © 1973, 1978, 1984, 2011 by Biblica, Inc.® Used by permission of Zondervan. All rights reserved worldwide. www.zondervan.com.

Proverbs 17:22 in chapter 25 is taken from the *Holy Bible*, New Living Translation, copyright © 1996, 2004, 2007, 2013 by Tyndale House Foundation. Used by permission of Tyndale House Publishers, Inc., Carol Stream, Illinois 60188. All rights reserved.

A Robertson Family Christmas is a work of fiction. Where real people, events, establishments, organizations, or locales appear, they are used fictitiously. All other elements of the novel are drawn from the authors' imaginations.

Library of Congress Cataloging-in-Publication Data

Robertson, Kay, date.
  A Robertson Family Christmas / Miss Kay Robertson ; with Travis Thrasher.
    pages cm
  ISBN 978-1-4143-9820-4 (hc)
1. Christmas stories. 2. Christian fiction. 3. Domestic fiction. 4. Duck dynasty (Television program)—Fiction. 5. Television personalities—United States—Fiction. I. Thrasher, Travis, 1971- II. Title.
  PS3618.O31697R63 2014
  813'.6—dc23   2014025656

Printed in the United States of America

20	19	18	17	16	15	14
7	6	5	4	3	2	

This book is dedicated to my grandchildren
and great-grandchildren.
They are the reasons I love Christmas so much!

"Well, you look about the kind of angel I'd get. Sort of a fallen angel, aren't you? What happened to your wings?"

A Letter from the Author

We receive letters weekly asking what it would truly be like to spend a day or two in West Monroe with my family. Since Christmas is one of my favorite times of year, I decided to set this Duck Commander work of fiction during that wonderful holiday.

When writing this novella, I knew I had to include a few of my favorite things: family, home-grown Louisiana cooking, and my Lord and Savior. I wondered what the Robertson family would look like to someone from a far-off city. While we love to have fun, especially around the holidays, we always keep our focus on the true meaning of Christmas.

Christmas is a chance to get together and laugh

and remember why we love one another. This book celebrates our true family holiday traditions while also imagining what a stranger might think of them. Especially if he had never heard of the Robertsons. I hope you enjoy this story, 'cause if there's one thing we love in the South . . . it's a tall tale.

Miss Kay

PROLOGUE

The first time Stacy Clarke saw the golden duck call, she thought someone was playing a cruel joke on her. It had been something she casually noticed on her iPhone while waiting in line at the bank. It popped up on her Facebook app in her messages, along with a note of congratulations and encouragement to check her e-mail. Soon she found herself in her car with her heart racing and her hand shaking, waiting to see what the message said.

She knew she couldn't read it in the bank. She didn't want anybody to watch her get emotional.

It had all started as a joke between her and a coworker. She worked at an investment firm as the office manager ever since she had gotten out

of the real estate business back in 2008. That
had been a particularly brutal time, with her job
imploding and her marriage exploding. Or maybe
it was the other way around. Either way, neither
survived the end of the year.

There were seven people who worked at
the investment firm, including her close friend
Deborah. One summer day during lunch, Stacy
had been telling her all about her youngest son's
issues. She wasn't sure if Hunter was depressed
or bored or suicidal or what. Her concern didn't
come from the pot she'd found in his bedroom
or from the time he stayed at a friend's house
all night without asking permission. It just came
from his overall blasé attitude about every single
thing in this world. She'd had enough.

"You should enter this contest I just found out
about," Deborah told her.

Joking, of course.

They both knew about the Robertson family,
and Stacy was actually a pretty big fan of them. It
wasn't like they could relate to a family of Loui-

siana rednecks. They were suburbanites living an hour west of Chicago in the small town of Appleton. But the beards and the hunting weren't the only foreign things that strangely attracted Stacy.

She loved the values the family had. She loved their beliefs. In a way they seemed naive in this tough and hard world, but this family was tough and hard. She couldn't get enough of the Robertsons and Duck Commander.

"They're having a contest where they'll pick a kid to spend Christmas with them."

"Are you serious?"

"Sure. Saw it on their Facebook page. You should tell Hunter to sign up. Give you some peace and quiet around the holidays."

Deborah had only been joking. And at first, Stacy hadn't given it any more thought. Surely it was for homeless and needy kids. Or really messed-up teens who needed some kind of outlet and a safe home for Christmas. But one night Stacy checked the contest out and realized it was open for anyone.

Anyone.

So without Hunter's knowledge she signed him up. Not really thinking or dreaming that he'd actually get picked.

But the golden duck call was the sign of the winner. That's what the contest information said:

WHOEVER WINS THE CHRISTMAS WITH THE ROBERTSONS WILL RECEIVE A GOLDEN DUCK CALL A FEW WEEKS BEFORE THE HOLIDAY.

It was crazy to think she'd won, because what were the odds? There was no way.

But what about your—?

She silenced her thoughts. No, it just wasn't going to happen. Things didn't happen like this.

There were stories for books and movies and songs and reality shows, but they were made up, like most of the hope in this world. They weren't real. Doors didn't actually open, not ones like this, not in this random of a way.

But you tried and you put your heart and story out there . . .

It was crazy to see her hand shaking like this. It wasn't like she was winning the lottery or something. It could be just a simple thing, really. Hunter could go down there against his will and have an okay time and simply come back with a new experience. Maybe a little different attitude. But was this a life changer? A game changer, as so many liked to say?

She exhaled, then opened the e-mail.

Another image of the golden duck call could be seen.

Hello, Stacy! We're so happy to congratulate you in welcoming Hunter to West Monroe this Christmas. After almost half a million entries, Hunter was chosen to be our special holiday guest! We're so excited to meet him and introduce him to all the Robertsons.

Attached is a document listing the specific details. I also am including my cell phone number for you to give me a call. I know it will be a big deal letting Hunter come down here. I'd love to just chat briefly over some things whenever you get a chance.

Thanks for trusting us with Hunter! We hope this is going to be something he always remembers and cherishes.

God bless and talk soon.
Korie Robertson

By the second paragraph, the tears were already falling.

It couldn't really be happening, could it?

Did you really put this together, God?

She'd prayed for this to happen. Not for herself. Not for her family. But for Hunter. The ache in her heart was something she carried around all day like a tight belt digging into her skin. The years had passed in a blink as everybody said they would. The little extroverted, energetic toddler who drove her mad had one day woken up a young man, with hair starting to grow on his face and a voice she didn't recognize.

Somewhere in between the toddler and the young man stood a Grand Canyon of grief. One she had to fly over every day. She knew that if she ever stopped and looked down, she'd fall. And it had been a long time since she lost her parachute.

The worry crept in, of course. Like it always did. What would Hunter say? How would he react? What about her ex? What about Carson, Hunter's older brother?

So many questions floated around without answers.

She knew she couldn't answer any of them right now. She would take them one at a time. Just like she had taken life a day at a time for over half a decade now ever since finding herself a single parent.

She would take one step and then another. Sometimes she wondered how many she'd be able to take, but then another day would be sinking away and she would realize she'd made it.

Stacy knew she wasn't the one giving herself strength. She just feared that Hunter would never realize that.

She closed her eyes and did the first thing that needed to be done. She thanked God.

Then, as she finally drove away from the bank, she began to try to figure out how and when she would tell Hunter.

He would definitely *not* be thankful. But then again, maybe any reaction from him would be better than what he'd become this past year.

She could hope.

Sometimes that's all anybody could do.

Hope and pray.

1
I WON'T BE HOME
for CHRISTMAS

Hunter held the plastic gift card like it was a business card from someone selling life insurance. On the front of it was the white Apple logo that matched his laptop and his iPhone and his "I" life. On the back was his name and $250 written in pen that had smudged so it was barely readable.

Hunter Clarke's father was speeding to get to the airport. Not because he might miss his flight but because Hunter might. And heaven forbid that might mean he had to stay home and actually spend Christmas with his family.

"That would stink if you got a ticket," Hunter told his father.

"I'd make your mother pay for it then."

This actually made Hunter laugh. "I'd like to see *that*."

The BMW switched two lanes without his father bothering to signal.

"I asked Stacy to take you since this was her idea to start with, but she said she couldn't leave work."

"I don't have to go."

His father let out an annoyed sigh. "We talked about this."

"I think Mom and you talked about it. Somehow I wasn't a part of the conversation."

Which was typical of how they operated. His entire life was dictated by others in another room. Who he'd stay with and where he'd go and what he'd do.

Sometimes he thought of the news story about the girl suing her parents. Sometimes he thought of trying that himself, but then again, he was only seventeen years old.

Maybe in another year I'll take 'em both to court. Failure to parent in any meaningful way. Emotional damages of a million dollars.

"You know I'll be with Carson over break."

"I could go too," Hunter said.

"Not this time," Dad said. "I told you—soon enough. We're gonna be busy, and I don't think you'd have much fun."

Hunter didn't say anything more. He'd already tried harder than usual. Most of the time he just kept his mouth shut when it came to Dad and his precious older brother. "Carson this" and "Carson that" and training and summer workouts and games and schedules and off-season and all that nonsense.

His older brother was born with the ability to catch a football and run. The only thing Hunter really caught in his life was a case of chicken pox or measles or rheumatic fever. The last one was quite a doozy, too.

But I'm very clever.

Hunter knew that football got you far in life. Being clever got you sent to the principal's office.

3

"I still think duck calls are made up," Hunter said. "They can't be real. A business built off making duck calls? Come on."

"Quite a successful business. See—you put your mind to it, you can come up with something like that."

"Obviously I have to. 'Cause it's not like my athletic abilities are gonna get me far."

Dad was way past the point of taking bait like this, but that didn't mean Hunter wouldn't still try. He thought of the evening when his mother told him about winning the contest. The first thing Hunter had ever won, and it was like sending him away to prison.

Louisiana? Duck hunting? Bearded men?

At first he had thought it was a joke, but he also knew Mom wasn't the joking kind. Then he simply told her no, he wasn't going to do it. It finally took getting Dad on the phone to make Hunter realize this was not something he could get out of. He had tried numerous times to tell them he wasn't going, but they made it very clear he was leaving.

"I really hate everything about this," Hunter said.

Dad's jaw tightened as he looked at him. "You're always telling me that you're tired of being at home, that you're tired of being around your mother."

Yeah, 'cause I want to be with Carson and you.

"This is your chance to get away."

"Spring break in Cancún is getting away," Hunter said. "This is just being gone."

Soon the BMW was parked alongside the curb outside the doors for American Airlines.

"Look, buddy, this is gonna be fun. Do you realize who you're spending Christmas with?"

"People keep telling me," Hunter said.

He hated when his father used the word *buddy*. Dogs should be called buddy, not youngest sons.

"Do you know I had two different fathers try to buy this off me?"

"I wouldn't have objected," Hunter replied. "We could have split the earnings. Not told Mom. Gone to an NFL play-off game."

He got a clap on the shoulder. "Think of this as some grand adventure."

"Yeah, okay."

"And hey—don't you go spending that gift card until you're with me," Dad said with a grin that reminded him of Carson.

"I won't."

"Merry Christmas."

It was three days before the actual day, so Hunter assumed he was supposed to wear these words on his chest like a name tag at some awful function.

"Tell Carson I said to break a leg," Hunter said.

Dad just shook his head. He hated that joke and so did Carson. They had a thing about being superstitious.

Hunter also had a thing about being super sick when it came to almost anything to do with Carson. Yet the truth was that if Dad asked him to go to Carson's university, Arizona State, and hang out with them for the next two weeks, Hunter would do it in a heartbeat.

He knew it would also probably be the two best weeks of his life.

He grabbed his backpack and suitcase and slipped out of the car. He headed through the sliding-glass doors and toward security. Dad had been nice enough to print off his boarding pass. So very thoughtful of him.

As he stood in line, Hunter saw a family of four waiting together and talking and laughing. He watched them more out of fascination than anything else.

The frustrating part of life wasn't the sadness he carried around like house keys in his pocket. It was standing at a closed door, knowing there was something better behind it.

Standing there and never, ever finding the right key to open it.

2
O LITTLE TOWN
of WEST MONROE

A storm was coming to West Monroe.

Korie Robertson looked out the window above her kitchen sink and saw clouds resembling a traffic jam of gray in the sky. The forecasters had said they might be getting some sleet or even snow later this week. She dried her hands and then checked the app on her phone that was tracking Hunter's flight. It was still scheduled on time, which was good. This was one of the busiest weeks of the year, so she was hoping and praying the weather didn't delay their Christmas guest. She had an hour-by-hour itinerary written out in her mind and she didn't want to have to scratch off anything.

The phone rang as if it knew she had a moment to talk. The Luke Bryan ringtone signaled that her husband was calling.

"Hey," Korie said.

"Everything still looking good?"

"So far."

"Is John Luke gonna ride with you to the airport?"

"Yeah. Bella too. But I haven't seen John Luke yet."

"He can't still be sleeping," Willie said. "Can he?"

"Well, it is Christmas break."

His last official Christmas break, too. At least his last official high school one.

"I hope the lunch goes well," she said. The Christmas lunch that Korie had planned for the warehouse employees was scheduled for today.

"We'll be fine. I'll call you if there's a problem."

"I hate to miss it, but I'm not about to let this kid show up in West Monroe with no one there to greet him."

"You don't even know what this guy looks like, do you? He could be part of a biker gang from Chicago, you know."

She shook her head and let out a slight laugh. "He's seventeen years old and lives in the suburbs."

"Do you know what the driving is like in Chicago? All that traffic? I'm just sayin'."

"It's a good thing Hunter's spending Christmas here, then."

"Yeah, well, let me know when you get him. And then check in with me every ten minutes. For safety's sake."

"Oh, hush." She sat down on the couch and noticed again how bare everything looked. "I can't wait to start decorating for Christmas."

"You were the one who wanted to hold off until he got here," Willie said.

"We always have so much fun decorating. You know that. I just thought it would be a good activity for the kids to do with Hunter. Kids tend to talk more when they're actually doing something together. Will you be able to get home a little early?"

The pause on the phone was unusual and very loud.

"What's up?" Korie quickly asked.

"Oh, nothing. I just—it all depends. There's a lot going on this afternoon. I'll text you."

The response piqued her curiosity. It wasn't anything that Willie said but *how* he said it that made Korie a little intrigued. When you've been married for over twenty years, you truly begin to think like your spouse. Grunts and sighs and laughs and unfinished sentences can communicate as much as words and phrases might. Sometimes even more.

"We have to allow enough time to decorate everything before heading over to your folks' for dinner."

"You really think we should bring this kid duck hunting?" Willie asked.

"Of course you should. It'll be something he'll never forget."

"As long as he doesn't shoot someone. By accident. Or on purpose."

She chuckled, then said good-bye to Willie

without overthinking anything more. Holidays always brought out the best and the worst in everything. Her husband was probably just busy like the rest of the world. Well, maybe a little more. When the rest of the world knew about you, life could become quite hectic. Lots of people were knocking on doors. To say the least.

Yet for one moment right now, the house was quiet. No knocks could be heard.

Korie closed her eyes for a second. *One day, this place will always be this quiet.*

She opened her eyes again and realized that yes, maybe this house could get more quiet down the road. But it also might hopefully get louder too. The addition of spouses and grandkids could really turn up the volume.

Not that I'm ready to be a grandmother just yet.

All in God's timing. It was something she had learned to trust. The unpredictable and often unlikely timing of events under God's control.

There were seasons in this life, a common phrase that she knew was absolutely true. But she also knew you couldn't do everything you wanted and be everything you wanted to be in each season.

Before checking on John Luke, she glanced at a family portrait on the wall from when John Luke and Sadie were toddlers. The rest of the kids were just glimmers in their imagination.

Something tugged on her heart, but she let it go for now. She knew what it was, and it was just part of life. Part of growing older. The natural progression of things.

She could fill this house and many others with all the things she was grateful for. So this Christmas was going to be just that. Another time to celebrate God's goodness and grace. Another chance to celebrate God's ultimate gift in the form of his only Son.

Korie let out a slight sigh.

I'm gonna be just fine. I know I will.

"I think I should bring back the mullet," John Luke said as he sat in the passenger seat of their SUV.

Bella giggled from the backseat.

"That was fun while it lasted," Korie replied with a smile. "But all good things must come to an end. Especially mullets."

Just like his father, John Luke loved having fun and making people laugh. Recently he'd decided to grow a mullet for a while. Korie finally had to intervene before things got out of control.

Rain fell on the windshield, but it was just a slight drizzle. The real problem was that cold front coming in later this week.

"Think we're gonna get snow for Christmas?" Bella asked.

"I hope so. It'd be fun to see it."

"The dude from Chicago gets to go to Louisiana for Christmas and we might get snow," John Luke said. "I'm sure he'll think it's hilarious how everything shuts down around here with even a hint of snow coming. Poor guy."

Korie flicked on the windshield wipers. "Maybe he's the one bringing it."

"What if that really happened?" John Luke said.

"What do you mean?"

"Well, I mean, what if this guy coming—?"

"Hunter."

"Yeah, what if when Hunter gets here, all these weird things start happening? It snows. And gets real cold. Then all the roads are gridlocked with crazy drivers . . ."

"You've been listening to your father, haven't you?" Korie said. "There's more to Chicago than the cold and the traffic."

"It's pretty flat there, right?" Bella asked.

"Yes, but it's got Lake Michigan. It's beautiful."

"I bet people aren't as friendly there," Bella replied, sounding suspicious.

Korie thought about her trips to Chicago and the surrounding area. "Midwesterners are more friendly than Northerners. But you know you can't judge people by putting them in some kind of box. What if everybody thought men with big beards who loved to hunt were dangerous?"

"You mean they aren't?" John Luke joked.

Bella joined in. "One day, in another ten or twenty years, I'll be dangerous too."

Laughter filled the car.

"You know," Korie said, "your father used to have a baby face like John Luke's. People can't get over what he looked like."

Bella grinned. "I think it'd be funny if this guy shows up today with a big beard and dressed in camo."

Soon they found themselves parked outside the small West Monroe airport. Korie liked it because it was so easy to fly in and out of. There were only a handful of gates and a small parking lot right next to it. They were accustomed to many early morning flights out of West Monroe and many late night flights coming back in.

Korie checked her phone to see if there were any messages. She had given Hunter her cell number in case anything came up. So far no message had come through.

As she read an e-mail, John Luke moved forward in his seat to look out the front windshield. Bella squinted out her window.

"Is that him?" John Luke asked.

Korie glanced at the tall figure exiting through the automatic sliding doors, a backpack slung over his shoulder and a small wheeled suitcase behind him. He stood on the curb, eyes fixed on the phone in his hand.

"I bet it is."

The first thing that stood out was the hair. Korie thought he had a modern James Dean vibe going for him with the short sides and the higher, textured front. His black military overcoat added to this impression. So did the matching style of boots.

Then there were the headphones he had around his neck. White Beats. As if he were a professional athlete walking into a stadium knowing all the cameras would be on him.

John Luke glanced at Korie and gave her a smile. Then all three of them hopped out of the vehicle.

"Hi, I'm Korie."

The guy looked up, pocketed his phone, and shook her extended hand. "Cool."

"And this is John Luke and Bella."

This time Hunter just gave nods without the handshake.

"Did you have a good flight?" Korie asked.

"I listened to Thirty Seconds to Mars the whole time."

"Thirty seconds to what?"

"It's a rock group, Mom," John Luke said.

"Oh." Korie laughed. "Well, good thing you got your suitcase."

"Was I not supposed to bring one?"

"No, just—long story."

She was used to teenage boys who might possibly leave their luggage at the baggage claim. John Luke had done this twice that she could remember.

"You can sit up front, Hunter," she said as they climbed back into the SUV.

Hunter hadn't done or said anything wrong, but Korie detected something standoffish in him. She thought it was his tone and his piercing glance that didn't waver.

Maybe he's just nervous. I'd be nervous if I were spending Christmas in a faraway place.

"So, Hunter, tell us a little about yourself."

"Really?"

He said this in an are-you-kidding-me? sort of way.

"Yeah—I mean, it's no big deal. Just wondering if you've ever been to West Monroe or to Louisiana."

"No and yes."

She forced a smile and looked at him. "So you have been to Louisiana?"

"Yeah."

"Whereabouts?"

"We came down to Mardi Gras a couple of years ago. Spent a week in New Orleans."

"Your whole family?"

"Just my dad and older brother. Weren't you supposed to get an overview about me? My parents are divorced."

"Right," Korie said. "But I wasn't sure about the timing. We didn't ask for a lot of info—we wanted to get to know you when you arrived."

She glanced in the rearview mirror to make sure John Luke and Bella were actually in the car. *You could help me out a little here, kids.*

"Well, you got someone pretty random with me," Hunter said.

She didn't understand what he meant by this but didn't want to push either.

"I'm glad you've been to New Orleans at least. Did you enjoy it?"

"No."

A simple and straightforward no. No explanation. No nothing.

"You didn't like New Orleans?"

"It smelled like pee," Hunter said. "Everybody was drunk. Including my father. It was actually hot. Sticky hot. Our hotel didn't have Wi-Fi or my dad didn't want to pay for it. I just wanted to get back home."

"That sure does stink," Korie said. "No pun intended. New Orleans is a great city. That's just a bad time to go there. But West Monroe is a little more laid-back. Right, guys?"

That was her kids' prompt.

"Right," John Luke said. Bella only nodded.

Going once . . . Going twice . . . Sold to the silent children in the backseat!

"We have you staying with John Luke in his room. He has a cot that you can sleep on. But tonight you'll be staying at Miss Kay and Phil's house."

"Who are they?"

She looked to see if Hunter was serious. "Those are Willie's parents. John Luke's grandparents."

"And we'll be sleeping there?"

She could tell that he didn't understand. "Ever been duck hunting?"

"No, but I hear that's what you folks do," Hunter said.

He made it sound like a strange practice. Like they were members of some weird cult in the deep woods.

"You'll love it," she said. "They leave early in the morning, so that's why you'll be staying with Phil and Miss Kay."

"Can't wait," he said in a way that suggested he surely could.

Hunter's gaze studied the passing countryside of West Monroe. Korie felt like she could have said almost anything and he'd have that same sort of look. Straight-faced without any emotion.

"We were thinking that this afternoon we would decorate the tree and our house. We wanted to wait until you were here to do it."

This would be the ideal time for Hunter to reply with something like "Wow, that's so nice of you to wait" or "That sounds like a lot of fun" or maybe even just an "Okay, cool."

Instead, Hunter said, "I'm not that great with decorating."

"It'll be easy," Bella said. "We tend to get silly, so you'll like it."

Korie forced a smile but already wondered if the edge of the cliff she stood on was crumbling. Her stomach twisted a bit like it did the time she, John Luke, Sadie, and Rebecca rappelled down the side of a twenty-four-story building. But in this case, the feeling was from going over the edge for another reason.

He's just a teenager who's probably anxious and uncomfortable.

"I promise you, we don't bite," Korie said to him with a smile that was natural, not forced. "Well, everybody except Uncle Si. He sometimes does, so be careful around him."

This prompted a smile, but that was all.

But it was a start.

Every good thing has a start in this life, she thought. *Even if it's slow and tedious. You always have to start somewhere.*

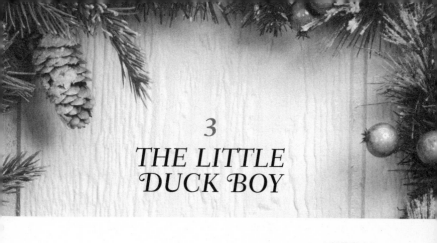

3
THE LITTLE DUCK BOY

Hunter was expecting a big farmhouse or maybe a mansion or something. Instead, they arrived in a subdivision not much different from his own back in Appleton, Illinois. The house they pulled up in front of was average, too. He assumed there might be mounted bears greeting them by the mailbox. Maybe a Confederate flag draped across the garage door. A giant duck hanging from the roof. This couldn't really be their house. It was way too typical.

"John Luke, why don't you show Hunter your room upstairs."

He followed John Luke into the house and upstairs. There were no dead ducks anywhere to be found. No men with beards. At least not yet. Everything felt strangely familiar.

When they got to John Luke's room, Hunter couldn't resist asking a question that he'd been wondering ever since he learned about winning the contest.

"Does your family really hunt?"

John Luke smiled and nodded. "Sure."

"The whole thing with the beards and all that— is all that real?"

"Are the beards real?" John Luke asked, chuckling a bit. "Yeah."

"I looked you guys up after learning I'd won the contest."

John Luke didn't respond. He was moving some clothes off a cot next to the wall.

"You know—I didn't even know about the contest."

"Really?" John Luke asked. "This is your bed, by the way. It's pretty comfortable."

There was an American flag on the wall over the cot. American, not Confederate. And on the wall behind John Luke's bed was a picture of the snowcapped Rocky Mountains.

"You like to ski?" Hunter asked.

"Uh-huh. And snowboard."

Hunter laughed. "So you do a lot of snowboarding around here?"

"No. But our family has taken some trips out west to Colorado."

"Yeah?" *Mine too. When we were a family. When Dad decided to include Mom and me in his life.*

"I'll get you a pillow and some blankets," John Luke said.

"Cool." Hunter placed his bags on the floor and his headphones and iPhone on the cot.

"The bathroom is right around the corner," John Luke said.

John Luke was nice. Like too nice. Like maybe there-can't-be-a-nicer-guy-on-the-planet sort of nice. Which made Hunter suspicious.

"Is your family really that rich?"

John Luke didn't react to the question. He simply shrugged. "I don't know. I mean—we're really fortunate. God's blessed us; I know that."

Hunter felt a dread come over him, a feeling of having to do something he really didn't want to do. Like seeing a plate of asparagus that he had to eat. Slimy and sickly and resembling alien fingers. Yes, that's exactly how he felt.

I don't ever want to eat asparagus, and I don't want God shoved down my throat, either.

It was gonna be a long week.

The sound of Christmas carols seemed to be coming from the ceiling. There was a lot of activity downstairs in the kitchen with people everywhere.

"Would you like something to drink?"

Hunter shook his head at Korie. "I'm fine."

There was laughter in the other room and conversation filling the house and a television on in the background and more people coming and going.

"It's a little crazy here," Korie told him. "I'll introduce you to everybody in a minute. Willie should be here in a short while."

"Sure." Hunter was beginning to realize that in spite of its average appearance, this house contained something that he couldn't relate to.

It was called life. Energy. Stuff happening. Movement and motion and electricity and excitement. And this was just in the afternoon.

He thought of his house and what it felt like every afternoon. It was like waking up an old, sleeping dog that quickly went back to bed. He'd arrive home while his mom was still working at the office. Sometimes he wondered if she really had to work or if it was just something she did to pass the time like he did playing games on his iPhone.

All these people made him nervous. But it was also interesting to see. Just lots of people and lots of motion and lots of everything.

There was a pretty girl walking around who had to be John Luke and Bella's sister since she looked so much like them. Then there was another pretty girl who looked older and a bit like a fashion model or something. She definitely didn't look like his sister. There were also some younger kids and some older folks.

I feel like a doorknob on an unused closet.

"John Luke, I think you need to make the introductions," Korie said. "You too, Bella."

Hunter wanted to say, *No, please, it's fine; I'd rather bury my head in the backyard,* but he remained silent. So John Luke and Bella took him around the large kitchen and then into another room with couches and chairs in it to formally introduce him to everybody. Hunter wanted to tell everybody that yes, he was the poor, homeless kid from Chicago who needed a family to spend Christmas with and show him love and warmth on this holiday. A part of him really wanted them to believe that, but he had a feeling they already knew he wasn't poor and homeless and all that. It still would've been funny.

The pretty girl was John Luke's younger sister,

Sadie. The fashion model was his older sister, Rebecca, who had to be adopted or something. Then there was Will, who didn't look like them either.

Why didn't I read more about their family?

He was introduced to Korie's parents, a friendly couple who asked him about Chicago and the weather and the flight and lots more questions. Then he was introduced to a few of Bella's friends, more of Korie's family, a Scandinavian cook, a hairdresser named Mohakalaka, and a personal trainer named BustYouUp.

Okay, maybe not the last three, but Hunter half expected them to show up after having his mind filled with all these introductions.

They were all so . . . friendly. So smiley. It was tiring. He didn't like smiling and didn't feel a need to smile. Not ever. But with all these people, he sorta felt like he needed to. They were paying attention to him. They genuinely seemed interested in him. And that just felt weird. He especially felt awkward around Sadie because most of the pretty girls he knew in his life avoided him like the plague. They didn't look his way and they didn't bother to wonder if he was going to say anything and they certainly didn't *smile* at him.

I hope I didn't blush when Sadie smiled at me.

He assumed he'd be going to a house full of people like his father. The kind who'd give you a gift card and a pat on the back and then say, "Knock yourself out" while walking away.

Hunter could take the pats on his back because they meant nothing. But the smiles and the handshakes and the interest seemed so genuine and felt so different.

After introducing him to Korie's brother, John Luke gave him a friendly smile. "Don't worry—we won't quiz you on the names."

Hunter wanted to tell John Luke thanks or that he hoped not. But he just nodded.

Sometimes the words were at the tip of his tongue, but he didn't have the courage to get them out. So they sank back into the dark well where he stored them.

There was a time when Hunter thought that well was going to overflow, that it couldn't possibly get any more full. But he knew now it was endless. And he also knew it was going to be there for the rest of his life.

4
SILVER and GOLD and CAMO

Willie was late. While this was nothing new, he hadn't answered the calls or texts Korie had sent. The warehouse said he'd taken off an hour ago.

Maybe he's sneaking off to buy some Christmas presents.

Her parents and extended family had gone home, leaving only the kids and Hunter. The smell of warm sugar cookies filled the kitchen. The fireplace was going in the family room since it was actually cold outside and it rarely got used. Korie loved the sound of fresh wood crackling and the sight of flames waving gently at her while she watched from the sofa.

She was ready to start decorating the tree with the family and their new guest, but she couldn't start without Willie.

"Do you guys know where your father might be?"

None of the kids knew. She was about ready to call him again when the door to the garage opened and Willie walked in.

"Oh yes," he shouted, looking at the two pans of cookies waiting for him. "Got here just in time."

"I was wondering where you were."

Willie gave her a kiss on the cheek before grabbing a couple sugar cookies. "Oh, I was handling a few last-minute things for Christmas."

"I have all the presents for the kids," Korie said.

Willie only nodded now that he had a full mouth.

"We still need to get some of the boxes with the decorations," she told him.

"These are great." Willie wolfed another cookie down and walked into the den, where the kids were.

Hunter was on the couch playing with his iPhone.

"So I assume you're the one from Chicago?" Willie asked.

Hunter looked up and nodded, then kept playing his game. Willie glanced back at Korie with a surprised grin on his face.

"I'm Willie. You are?"

"Hunter."

"Serious?" Willie asked.

"About what?"

"That's your name?"

"Yeah," a completely disinterested Hunter said.

"So do you actually hunt?"

"No. Do you actually will things to be?"

Willie stood there thinking for a minute. "Ha, that's a good one."

It didn't look like Hunter was trying to be funny, however.

"Did they give you a tour?" Willie asked Hunter.

"I showed him around," John Luke said.

"Good. Did you warn him about all the things that were going to happen the next few days?"

This got Hunter's attention. He looked up again and put down the phone.

"You ever see *Christmas Vacation*?"

"Yeah," Hunter said.

"Hey, Korie, you didn't tell me he actually could speak!"

Hunter still wasn't smiling.

"Well, our home is a bit like that during the holidays. The wild family and the squirrels in the tree and the insane brother. We got all that. Has he met Uncle Si?"

"Not yet," Sadie said.

"Oh, boy, you're in for a treat."

Hunter didn't say anything else, so Willie seemed to let him be. He walked back to the kitchen area, where he raised his eyebrows at Korie.

"He's friendly," he said under his breath.

"He's been that way ever since picking him up," Korie replied.

The music was loud enough for them not to be heard.

"Is this kid some kind of troubled teen or something?"

"No, I don't think in the traditional sense," Korie said. "His parents are divorced—that's all I really know."

Glancing at him now, finger tapping away at his smartphone, they could see he looked pretty typical.

"Is he depressed? On meds? Did they pack a dozen bottles for him?"

"Be nice," Korie said.

"What was I just doing?"

"Come on—let's get the rest of the boxes for the tree."

Korie knew people who paid professionals to come and decorate their house for Christmas. Some of those friends had even suggested that she use them, but that wasn't for her. Ever since she could remember, they'd been decorating the Christmas tree themselves using the handmade ornaments the kids had crafted when they were younger. Once the lights and garland were on, the ornaments filling the tree would create a hodgepodge of almost everything. But to Korie, the Christmas tree held a hundred snapshots from their past. Snapshots she loved seeing again since it reminded her of the children being younger.

They grow up so fast, and don't let anybody tell you anything otherwise.

She watched the kids going through boxes, getting ready to start hanging their decorations. Willie and John Luke were in charge of the lights, and after that it was a free-for-all. The sound of their laughter made her ache just a bit. She knew it wouldn't always be like this. They might slow down growing taller but they would continue growing older and becoming independent and living their own lives. They would go on to hopefully start new families on their own.

"They'll leave us behind so we can lose our marbles together in a nursing home."

She smiled thinking of this comment Willie had made recently. He'd been joking that the kids would all grow up and move out and they'd become just like that couple from *The Notebook*. He'd read her their love story and she wouldn't remember it, and then he'd frighten her because he'd put lots of hunting stories and Robertson family stories in the book he was reading. She'd tell him he was crazy and he would say, *Yes, but that's why you love me.* Then she'd flip out and hit him over the head and leave. *The Notebook 2* starring Willie and Korie Robertson.

While the kids were sorting through the boxes, Korie walked past Hunter. "I think we all need to give Hunter a few of your ornaments."

"Tell Sadie," Rebecca said. "She's the one that has the most."

"It's unfair, too," Will said to Hunter.

The newcomer was staring and looking a bit like a kid lost in the woods.

"We have a tradition that all the kids decorate the tree with ornaments they've made."

41

"Like this," John Luke says, showing an ornament made with macaroni noodles.

"Now for some reason, it seems that John Luke ended up making a lot more ornaments than the others when he was younger," Korie said, trying to fill Hunter in on what was taking place.

"It's because you love him more," Sadie said, looking Hunter's direction, trying to get a smile or a reaction.

"That's why a few years ago, Sadie made some more ornaments," Korie said. "Just so she'd have the most."

"I don't know what they're talking about," Sadie said.

"It's true," John Luke said. "Look at her box." He grabbed a big heart ornament. "This was definitely not made by a first grader."

The handwriting was way too neat and the coloring was perfect.

"Hunter, you can have some of these." John Luke gave a box to Hunter that Korie hadn't seen. The look on his face told her he was up to something.

The kids soon began to decorate the tree. For a while it was a bit of creative chaos, accompanied by Bing Crosby and Perry Como and Burl Ives and all the Christmas classics.

Some things in life just needed accompaniment. The smell of sugar cookies and smoke from a nearby fire needed a Christmas tree. The pine tree needed the lights and garlands and decorations. And the act of placing ornaments on the tree needed the echoes of Elvis and Josh Groban and Judy Garland.

The kids were all laughing and joking while Korie watched and took pictures. She noticed Hunter staying on the couch, ignoring the tradition.

"Come on, Hunter; you can put some up too," Willie said, trying to encourage the teen.

Hunter nodded but remained indifferent, watching the others have fun.

I'm not going to force him to do anything. I can't make him hang an ornament nor can I make him happy enough to crack a smile.

"Hold on!" Sadie was standing in front of the

tree, her hands up like a traffic cop ordering cars to stop. "What is this?"

She held up an ornament Korie had never seen before. It had a picture of John Luke from when he was about seven years old with the words *Favorite Child* under the photo.

John Luke burst out laughing.

"Did you make more ornaments for yourself?" Sadie asked.

"I'd never do something like that."

John Luke was totally full of it.

Sadie rushed over to the box in front of Hunter and took out a handful of fake ornaments. "You made yourself another twenty ornaments!"

"What?" John Luke said. "Hunter, those look real, don't they?"

Even Hunter found it a bit funny. He smiled and nodded.

"No way," Sadie shouted. "Look at this. Come on!"

The ornament had a picture from John Luke's prom.

"This is from this year!"

"Maybe I used a time machine when I was in first grade to get that," John Luke said.

"See, Hunter," Willie said. "This is what happens with John Luke and Sadie. When everyone knows our favorites are really the youngest ones, Will and Bella."

The rest of the kids shouted at Willie. Nothing unusual for this gang. But Korie could tell Hunter wasn't used to it. His wide eyes were on them while his lips said nothing.

"Hey, it's only going to get louder and wilder," Korie whispered to him. "So get used to this."

She expected a smile or a chuckle or something. Anything.

Instead, Hunter nodded and looked like someone had told him his dog had died.

No, take that back. He probably wouldn't care if his dog died. Not this kid.

Their work was cut out for them, for sure. But she wasn't going to push and she wasn't going to try too hard. Things always come best when they're natural and they fall into place.

Be patient and loving. Just show love the Robertson way—with lots of laughter and lots of fun—and maybe Hunter will come around.

Maybe.

5
WAY TOO
HOLLY JOLLY
for CHRISTMAS

There was always that point in the Christmas season when Hunter started getting tired of all the songs and the decorations and the everything about it. This usually happened a week before December 25. The same sort of thing was happening to him at the Robertsons'.

Surely the happiness surrounding him was some kind of trick, an illusion performed for the sake of the newcomer. Hunter knew some families who got along, and he had some friends who actually didn't mind their parents or siblings. But it was nothing like this.

These guys had fun. It was as if . . . they actually *liked* each other.

The hilarity and games they played and the laughter they let loose with reminded him of overloading on some kind of dessert. It left him with a stomachache. Yet in this case, it was because he felt empty, his gut hollow and craving.

For what, he didn't know because Hunter didn't want *that*. All that over-everything in the family room. Overdoing the fun. Oversharing. Overseeing. He had caught a bad case of being overcome. He just wanted this Christmas holiday to be over.

Thankfully he could manage to be filled a bit by the loud rock music pounding against his head. They had about half an hour before they'd leave for the grandparents' house, so he lay down on the cot in his clothes, just staring at the ceiling fan and occasionally closing his eyes. He wasn't tired, however. Hunter felt restless and irritated and itchy with a carved-out soul left to scratch.

A simple contest. I bet I was randomly chosen.

There wasn't a reason he was here, in this room, with these people. There were no strings that had been pulled. There was no divine plan waiting to happen. Fate forced him to come down here the same way it forced him and Mom out of his brother's and father's lives. The random, ridiculous thing called life.

He turned the music up a little louder to get rid of those thoughts. Soon enough he'd be back home, back to the echoes left by his footsteps, back to turning on the lights in the evening by himself. Back to his familiar life.

But sometimes the songs weren't loud enough to drown out his mind.

This was a truth he knew all too well.

A nudge on his arm made him jump. It was John Luke.

He took off the headphones without stopping the blasting song.

"You doze off?" John Luke asked.

Hunter shook his head. "Are we leaving now?"

"No. Just wanted you to know there's a towel

and washcloth if you need something. Don't know if you take showers in the morning or night."

John Luke was so earnest. So much so that Hunter wanted to ask if he was being serious. But he knew the guy was being serious.

"We don't take showers in Chicago," Hunter joked.

"Oh yeah?" John Luke let out a laugh. "Bet everyone smells around there, then."

Hunter laughed himself, but he couldn't help it. "You've got a funny accent," he told John Luke.

"You kinda got an accent too."

"People from the Midwest don't have accents. We talk normal." Hunter turned off the music and put the iPhone in his backpack.

"They sounded loud," John Luke said.

"Yeah. It's a band called Muse. You should see them live." Hunter thought for a minute. "Go to many concerts?"

"Yeah, every now and then. Just saw Needtobreathe in concert."

"Never heard of him."

They heard Korie calling them from downstairs.

"I guess we should get going." John Luke grabbed something from the shelf by his bed.

"Any chance I can just stay here?"

"You'll like my grandparents. They're pretty cool."

"My grandmother's got Alzheimer's and my grandfather has lung cancer," Hunter said in a no-nonsense sort of way. "The others are dead."

"Sorry to hear that."

"Yeah. Life is full of a bunch of *sorrys*."

Hunter grabbed his headphones and backpack and headed toward the stairs. He had to get back in the mode of dealing with meeting new people who'd shake his hand and probably feel sorry for him. The loser who wasn't with his family for Christmas. Maybe Hunter could stop by a local Walmart and ask one of those people from the Salvation Army for their bell and bucket. Then he'd just start ringing the bell everywhere he went and holding out the bucket to every new stranger who tried to shake his hand.

That would keep them away. It would stop their conversations and keep them from prying.

"Ready to go?" Willie asked at the foot of the stairs.

"Yeah."

And he was ready.

Ready to go back home to Chicago.

Ready to be back at his house in sweet silence.

6
IT'S *the* (AL)MOST WONDERFUL TIME *of* THE YEAR

First there was the slightly awkward car ride from the airport, the kind where Korie kept thinking, *He's probably just a bit shy; surely that's all.* Then there was the couch-potato act back there at home while decorating the tree. Or maybe Hunter was trying to do an impersonation of Eeyore from *Winnie-the-Pooh*. She had hoped, however, that things would get lighter, especially going over to see Phil and Miss Kay.

Who *didn't* love Phil and Miss Kay?

It turned out that Hunter didn't even know much about them.

And then he decided to continue the whole bored-out-of-his-mind act at Phil and Miss Kay's house.

And that was just the start.

Phil had greeted Hunter while wearing camo pants and a camo T-shirt. This was his typical outfit. He was barefoot and resting in his favorite recliner while watching the news.

"Are we going hunting now?" Hunter had asked Phil.

Phil didn't miss a beat, however. "Is your real name Hunter?"

"Yeah."

"Then surely you do what your name says and *hunt*."

Hunter shook his head.

"So I shouldn't assume that one *hunts* if their name is *Hunter*? Correct?"

"Uh, yeah."

Phil nodded. "Then maybe you shouldn't assume that one is going hunting just because they're wearing camouflage in the safety of their home."

This had been their initial conversation. And with each subsequent one, it didn't appear as if communication was going to get any better.

Yet a strange thing had also happened. Hunter was becoming more vocal for some reason.

Miss Kay tried to make Hunter feel at home by greeting him and asking him what kind of food he liked. Hunter shrugged, didn't say much, and simply stared around the kitchen as if he was smelling something bad.

"I hear y'all have good pizza up there where you're from," Miss Kay said.

"Chicago deep-dish?" Hunter asked in mock surprise. "Yeah, it's pretty good."

"What other kinds of food do you like?"

"Let's see—bratwurst, Italian beef, hot dog. That's all people from *Chicauwgo* eat."

Korie decided to curb the conversation by asking Kay what she was making for dinner tonight.

"We are having fried shrimp," Miss Kay said.

That's what was in the deep cast-iron skillet on the stove.

"We'll also do some coleslaw and potato salad and fried okra."

"I don't eat fish," Hunter said as he stood at the island.

"Well, technically shrimp aren't fish," Korie said.

"Well, I don't eat seafood."

"Do you have food allergies?" Miss Kay asked.

"Yeah. I'm allergic to anything you have to pull out of water and then fry up or boil on a stove."

The guys were talking in the family room yards away from them. The rest of the family members—Jase, Jep, Alan, and their wives and kids—were all at their homes and busy doing their own thing. Everybody saw each other a lot throughout the year, and the mornings around Christmas were often devoted to duck hunting. So this time of year, the Robertson families only all got together in the afternoon on Christmas Day for a big meal and to open presents.

Korie tried getting Willie's or John Luke's attention in order for them to hopefully take Hunter and his attitude away. To maybe take a break on the couch or something. But Hunter certainly didn't seem to bother Miss Kay.

"You will have to try at least one shrimp," she told him in her most charming way.

"I don't know."

"Have you ever had okra?"

"Is that a fish?"

Korie couldn't help but laugh. It took her a second to realize Hunter wasn't joking.

"You've never had okra?" she asked.

"Deep-dish pizza, yes. Okra, no."

"Then you'll have to promise to try some okra, too," Miss Kay said.

Hunter might be strong but he wasn't strong enough for Miss Kay. He gave her a nod.

To Hunter's credit, he *did* try the fried shrimp along with the okra when they were finally sitting at the table for the meal. He admitted that he actually did like fried shrimp (and come on—who could seriously *not* love Miss Kay's fried shrimp?). The okra he wasn't a big fan of.

"Hunter, what sort of Christmas traditions do

you have in the great big Windy City on the lake?"
Phil asked.

For a moment, Hunter just looked at Phil and
the rest of them. Korie finally noticed something
that had been bugging her all day. *He almost never
smiles.*

She had seen it pop up maybe once or twice,
and it was actually a very likable sort of smile, but
usually he had a serious or distant look on his face
just like he did now.

"Well, I'm here, right?" Hunter said. "So I think
it's safe to say our family—the Clarkes—don't have
wonderful Christmas traditions like duck hunting."

"That's not a holiday tradition," Willie said.
"That's just a way of life."

"Do you actually live in Chicago?" Miss Kay
asked.

"No. We live in Appleton, which is west of the
city. About an hour away. I can't even remember
the last time I was in Chicago."

"I've loved Chicago every time I've visited,"
Korie said.

She didn't want the conversation to turn to his parents. She could easily see Hunter going on (or likely going off) about his mother and father being divorced. Thankfully Willie and Phil started to talk about tomorrow's hunt and the weather and typical Robertson men conversation.

"Do you think you'll be able to shoot a duck?" Phil asked Hunter.

"I'm not sure," Hunter said. "What if it doesn't want me to?"

Willie burst out laughing at that response. It was so natural and so normal. But Korie didn't know Hunter well enough to know if his response meant he was teasing or secretly mocking Phil.

Phil wasn't bothered. Nothing could rattle her father-in-law.

"You know what worries me about this country of ours?" Phil asked in a rhetorical sort of way. "It's that some people are up in arms about killing animals. They say meat is murder while they eat their hamburgers at the fast-food places. Yet they don't seem to care about taking God out of our schools.

They don't seem to *mind* our crumbling morality, our disintegrating marriages. Our overall moral decay."

Uh-oh. Phil's gonna start preaching.

Hunter didn't look freaked out, however. He seemed a bit amused. "Look, Mr. Robertson," he started.

"It's Phil."

"Yeah, well, Phil—I'm happy to kill a duck or two. I don't have any problems with that."

"Okay, then," Phil said.

"If you had said, 'Meat is murder,' we were gonna have to throw you in the swamp," Willie said.

Hunter laughed.

He actually laughed. Out loud. In an LOL sort of way.

No way.

Maybe it was the spirit of the Robertsons that was finally chiseling away at him. Bit by bit. The Robertson boys could break you like that. Not in a bad way but rather in the best sort of way possible. They chipped away with jokes and smiles and tough love. They were relentless fools but the kind you could not hate.

I'm biased, but it's still the truth.

"We have lots more shrimp," Miss Kay offered to Hunter.

He thought for a minute and looked around and then nodded. This got a big round of applause from half the table.

It was a nice sound to hear.

7
HARK! the
HERALD PHIL SINGS

For a moment, Hunter forgot the year and who he happened to be and imagined he was talking to some soldier from the Civil War. That's how crazy ridiculous he suddenly felt in the middle of this conversation with Mr. Robertson. Or Phil, as most everyone, including his son Willie, called him.

Phil was now telling Hunter his life story, and it was pretty wild. Hard to believe, but the guy actually told him he once played football and was a quarterback and then he quit to go hunting. He also said his backup was Terry Bradshaw.

*I'm not a football guy, but I know Terry Bradshaw,
so come on. You're saying Terry Bradshaw sat on the
bench behind you?*

Then Phil told Hunter a story about being
on the run from the law and how God found
him after he left his family. Smelling the sweet
aroma of Miss Kay's carrot cake, seeing the small
and messy TV room with the cozy couches they
sat on, Hunter found it hard to imagine Phil as
some abusive drunkard. Especially since he kept
quoting Bible verses.

"One of the worst mistakes of my life was opening that honky-tonk in the country."

"A honky-what?" he asked.

"A bar," Willie said, watching the television.

Hunter imagined that Willie had heard this
story once or a thousand times before.

"Oh, young Phil got himself into some trouble,"
Phil said as if he were talking about another person. "But Miss Kay and the boys took me back
in. And you want to know something, Chicago
Hunter? God gives you second chances. And

third chances. And fourth ones. He doesn't give up on you. I was twenty-eight years old and God still hadn't given up on me."

Hunter wasn't sure what this all meant, as he continued to listen to Phil talk about being baptized and baptizing others and all this. He wasn't sure if he meant baptizing like the kind they did in *The Godfather* with the baby. Or maybe a baptism in a bathtub or something like that. Hunter didn't know but didn't want to say, *Yeah, sure, sounds great, but what's this baptizing you're talking about?*

"You and your family attend church?" Phil eventually asked.

"It's just my mom and me," Hunter said. "My mom started to."

"But you don't have time."

"No, I have time," Hunter said. "I just think it's boring."

Willie looked up from his phone and grinned at Hunter.

"Let me show you something, Chicago Hunter," Phil said. He got up from his recliner and picked up some kind of book with pieces of paper hanging out of it.

He gave it to Hunter. It was heavy but also made of a soft leather.

"Think about it, Chicago Hunter," Phil said. "Think about a way *to leave the planet Earth*. Not leaving your house but leaving here, this whole planet. Does that sound boring?"

Hunter shook his head. "No."

"The answers are in this book. It's my favorite. And I keep wearing the pages out reading it."

Hunter knew enough to know this was a Bible.

"You know—I tell this to everybody," Phil said. "One day you're gonna be six feet under. I'm gonna be six feet under."

"I'll be six feet under too," Willie added without even looking up.

"So tell me something, Chicago Hunter. Does being buried six feet under sound *boring* to you?"

"Sounds depressing."

"Might be depressing to some. Or maybe it could be the most glorious start of the rest of *eternity*."

Hunter didn't know what to do. Sit still and open the Bible or put the Bible down and start running and get out of there.

"Here's the thing—this book tells the Good News. *Good* News. Not the kind that says it's gonna be a sunshiny day tomorrow or that you're gonna be rich or that you're gonna be happy. But this—this is the Good News. Our God who created me and you and everybody else actually gave his Son to us. For us. This whole Christmas thing. That's the Good News because Jesus was born."

Hunter didn't know what to say. He felt warm and uncomfortable and annoyed and awkward. He also felt silent for some reason.

Phil took the Bible back from him. "It's a simple story, really. Jesus came." He pointed down. "He died and was buried. Then Jesus rose from the dead, and after that he went to heaven." Phil pointed up. "But one day . . ." He pointed down again. "One day he's coming again. This is the simple story of Jesus. That sound boring to you?"

Hunter wanted to shrink into a ball on the

couch. Instead, he shook his head but didn't say anything.

"I think it's the very *opposite* of boring. There's nothing boring about death and the Resurrection and eternity."

Phil took the remote and found a movie on. "Just like this—Jason Bourne. You ever seen these movies?"

"Yeah," Hunter said.

"Now he's a cool cat. He can do anything. Get out of any jam. He's amazing. Isn't he cool?"

"Sure," Hunter said.

"Unfortunately, Bourne's made up. The amazing thing—the great news about the Good News—is that Jesus isn't made up."

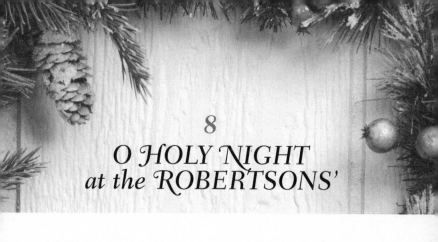

8

O HOLY NIGHT
at the ROBERTSONS'

"How's he doing?"

Korie couldn't help calling Miss Kay to check up on their new guest from the Midwest. It was around ten and she'd been back home for over an hour.

"Oh, he's doin' fine," Miss Kay answered. "I showed him how to make some carrot cake earlier. He'd never tried it. Can you believe it?"

"Did he like it?"

"Well, of course he did."

This made her feel a little better. Leaving him with Phil and Miss Kay had given her second thoughts. She knew they could handle anyone or anything thrown their way. She was more worried about Hunter and his attitude. He might say something or do something and then get a dose of Phil at his best.

For some strange reason Hunter doesn't seem intimidated by Phil.

She loved her father-in-law and couldn't imagine life without knowing him. His testimony was such a bright light in this dark world, and his outspokenness was just part of his unique character. There were parts of Willie that she knew absolutely came from Phil. But she also recalled how nervous she'd felt being around him when she and Willie were first dating. And even now she was aware how imposing he could seem with his beard and his long hair and his eyes often hidden behind those shades.

"Does he know about being quiet at night?" Korie asked. "I told him once but maybe just remind him again before you guys go to bed."

"Oh, we'll be fine. You don't need to worry."

She still could remember one night as a teenager having a sleepover at Phil and Kay's house.
It was a lot like it still looked now. Willie had told
her not to be loud at night. But the group had
been talking and laughing late into the evening
when suddenly they heard Phil coming out of his
bedroom. Korie had hidden under a blanket on
the couch, her heart racing and her breath held. It
turned out Phil was just getting something to drink.
But perhaps it had been a subtle (or maybe not-so-
subtle) warning to all of them. *Especially* Willie.

"What are they doing right now?"

"They're all watching a movie. You'd never guess
which one."

"Hmm. Let's see. Does it involve a spy who for-
gets who he is? Does his last name begin with a *B*?"

"Exactly," Miss Kay replied.

Phil and his love of Jason Bourne movies. Holly-
wood needed to make a few more just to appease
Phil's love of the films. *Bourne Is Back Again*.
Bourne Better Than Ever. Maybe even make a
Bourne Commander where Jason Bourne lost his

memory again and wound up working at Duck Commander.

"What's Willie up to?"

"He's over there laughing at something with the boys. Wanna talk to him?"

"Sure."

Willie got on the phone and greeted her.

"How's he doing?"

"Who? Hunter?"

"Well, I'm not wondering about John Luke. I haven't done that since he was, what . . . five?"

"Oh, it was bad," Willie said.

The temporary hope inside her popped like a balloon. "What happened?"

"You know Phil—he starts talking about the birds and the bees, and well . . ."

"What?" Korie said in disbelief.

There was a pause and her stomach continued to sink. "Tell me."

Willie just started laughing. "Oh, nothing. Come on."

"Are you kidding?"

"Everything's fine. You're worrying too much."

"That was mean."

He kept laughing. "I haven't seen you this nervous in a while."

"I'm not nervous. I just—I want this to be a special time for Hunter."

"Look, you know teens. You can't force good moods. You can't make them understand or see your way. You just gotta let things happen."

Willie. The voice of reason.

The truth was that many people really didn't know the wisdom behind the goofball. His humor (along with his beard) sometimes hid some really beautiful things about her husband.

"You know what I told you about Hunter . . ." Korie let her voice trail off.

"And you know what I said back."

"Maybe something about not worrying."

"Yeah, I think something like that."

"Just don't get anybody shot tomorrow," Korie said. "At least anybody *not* related to us."

"Hey—it was your idea to go duck hunting."

"Will Jase and Uncle Si be joining you?"

"Should be. They said they were coming."

Korie wondered what Hunter would think of meeting Uncle Si.

"You might want to warn him about Si," she told Willie.

"Surprises make the world go round."

"We don't want to scar the kid for life."

"Yes, we do," Willie said. "We want him to go back home clinging to his parents and begging them never to let him leave again."

"You're terrible."

"I gotta go. Bourne's about to go off on some bad guys."

Like father, like son.

Some things you're just *bourne* with.

9
I BETTER NOT HEAR WHAT I HEAR

"Turn that down," John Luke said.

For some reason, it seemed like everybody was terrified of waking up Phil.

He's an old man. Shouldn't he be sleeping like a log or something? Especially after all that preaching earlier?

Hunter knew that every time he saw his grandfather, the old guy would fall asleep in his favorite chair. They'd catch him with his mouth half-open and drool coming out with an occasional snore. Then he'd cough and open his eyes and adjust

75

himself in his chair before promptly falling back to semiconsciousness.

"Seriously it's too loud."

They were watching a James Bond movie that Hunter hadn't seen for a while. John Luke had told him he might want to go to sleep 'cause they had to wake up early. Then John Luke said to change the channel from the comedy that was on. Now he was telling Hunter to turn down the volume.

"It's not that loud."

Sometimes his mother would tell him to turn down the surround sound Bose speakers in the basement that would blast whatever the television was playing, but most of the time she left him alone to watch whatever he wanted to. It felt like the television was practically on mute right now.

"I'm serious," John Luke said.

So serious and so sweet about being so serious.

"Come on, it's not that bad. Look—I love this part." Hunter decided to adjust the volume. Making the Bond movie *louder*.

"Hunter, that's way too—"

Light from the hallway leading to Phil and Kay's bedroom suddenly spilled into the family room. John Luke stopped midsentence and looked that direction as if he were seeing a ghost.

Look—it's the Ghost of Christmas Past!

Hunter found this amusing. He even smiled as he kept watching the movie. Then he glanced toward the hallway and saw something that didn't make him smile.

In fact, the sight made him jump and sit up on the couch. For a second he forgot to breathe. He wondered if he was actually dreaming.

A tall, bearded figure wearing only boxers stood at the end of the hallway. Hunter wasn't sure, but he thought the figure was holding something. *A machete?* The kind that crazed killers carried around with them right before they started hacking away at teenagers?

Forget fearing the beard. I'm fearing the machete in his hand.

Hunter swallowed and grabbed the remote

and turned off the movie, plunging the room into darkness.

The figure moved from the hallway to the kitchen and opened the fridge. The light illuminated his face—sure enough, it was Phil getting out the water pitcher. But there was no machete in sight.

My imagination must have tricked me. Hunter couldn't remember the last time his heart had beat this fast. Or the last time he'd felt like throwing up from the fear squeezing the lining of his stomach.

The fridge closed and Phil disappeared. Like a ghost in the night. Or a serial killer changing his mind.

Any second now, Hunter expected to hear John Luke whisper something like "I told you so." But he didn't hear anything except the ticktock from the grandfather clock nearby.

He finally was able to breathe normally again. Maybe this would be a funny story to tell down the road, but for now, it was pretty terrifying. A lot more terrifying than anything he could have seen on television. No matter *how* loud it might be.

"Get up."

It was literally the world's worst wake-up call *ever*. This thick, heavy, very awake voice telling him to get up in a way that sounded like he might be smothered to death if he didn't. Hunter started to reach for the side of the bed and then realized he was on the couch just before he landed hard on the floor.

When he finally looked toward the kitchen, he could see John Luke standing there. Phil was behind him pouring some coffee into a thermos. It was surely Phil who had "encouraged" him to wake up.

"What time is it?" he asked John Luke.

"Three forty-five."

"Do you hunt ducks at night?"

John Luke chuckled. "We try to get out to the duck blind by five or five thirty."

"Because they won't be there at like ten or so?" Hunter muttered.

"Time to change," Phil said to Hunter as he walked past. "We don't want to wait around."

Something told Hunter that Phil didn't wait around much. And that the Robertson men didn't wait around much in general. The only things moving slow here were their beards, and those were pretty fast-moving too.

Several moments later, Hunter stepped into the dimly lit family room wearing the camouflage pants and coat he'd recently bought. They were so new he had just popped off the tags on both of them. For some reason, however, the guys all stood there giving him a funny look.

"Chicago, what is that?" Phil asked.

He looked at his coat as if something might be crawling on it. Or maybe something got spilled over it. But he couldn't find anything.

"What?"

"That," Phil said. "That kind of camo."

"You do know that it's not *snowing* where we're going," Willie said. "Right?"

"Yeah."

"Well, that camo is a little different from ours. Wouldn't you say?"

Hunter did notice that his coat and pants seemed to have more white in them than the others. A whole lot more white.

"That's snow camo," Willie said.

"For hunting in Alaska," Phil added.

"Camo that you use for hunting in the *snow*," Willie said.

They were having a lot of fun with this.

Hunter stared at his new outfit again. He could remember asking his mother if she thought this was the right kind. He'd already felt stupid enough shopping in the hunting section at the sporting goods store, so he wasn't about to ask one of the guys working there for any suggestions. He had just wanted to get it over with.

And that's why I ended up getting snow camo.

"I can still wear this; it's fine," Hunter said.

"Uh, no," Phil said.

"We have extra camo. They might smell like dead animals, but that's okay." Willie left to get Hunter another outfit.

"It's fine, really," Hunter kept saying.

"No, it's not fine, Trapper," Phil said. "It's white, and that's not fine."

Ten minutes into the car ride to the backroads of nowhere, Hunter felt like his nose was on fire.

"This smells horrible," Hunter said from the backseat of the big truck, which was covered in camo wrap.

They drove in darkness. Silence, mostly, too. But Hunter couldn't take any more of this.

"It smells worse than a dead animal," Hunter said.

John Luke laughed in the shadows next to him.

"Oh, I've smelled worse," Willie said as he drove the vehicle. "You should smell Uncle Si's hunting attire. The combination of stink and body odor and age makes for a terrible trio."

"It can't get any worse than this."

"It can always get worse," Phil said. "Trust me."

Phil's words were a little like the old guy at the start of a horror movie who tells the couple or the kids or the whoever to not go there. *Don't go spend the night at the haunted house,* or *Don't go to the cabin in the woods,* and definitely *Don't go swimming in the lake.* And the old guy was always right because it could and usually did get worse.

Hunter was about to discover the truth in these words when they got out of the truck.

"You ever shot a gun before?"

Hunter held the rifle like it was some kind of alien newborn in his arms. "I usually take my M16 to target practice every Wednesday."

"You have an M16?" Phil said in complete shock.

"It's sarcasm," Willie said. "That's funny. I take that as a no."

"You take that right."

"So here's my instructions," Phil said. "Keep the safety on. That's this little button. Don't shoot until you're told."

"You'll tell us?"

"You'll see when. Don't shoot anybody else. Kill the ducks. End of instructions."

"That's it?" Hunter asked.

"Just poke that gun out there in the air and fire till you see 'em drop. Doesn't matter how you do it; we just want to see them die. That's it."

Okay, then.

"I wish you were my chemistry teacher," Hunter said, not really joking at all.

"Some things in life are better learned by doing than talking."

The air felt crisp, much like it might back home in the Chicago suburbs. Hunter could see his breath. He actually drank some of the coffee in the thermos simply to warm up. Then he looked over and saw Phil putting something on his face.

"You really don't want those ducks to see you, do you?" Hunter said.

"That's the plan," Phil replied. "You're pretty pale yourself. You could use some of this."

"Well, I do have this wonderful Duck Commander cap I'm wearing. I need some DC shades now."

"We got those," Willie said.

"How about Duck Commander camo?"

"You're wearing it."

Maybe it was because he was so tired, or maybe it was from the coffee he'd sipped (and Hunter never drank coffee), but he suddenly felt like being a real smart guy.

"Do you have Duck Commander boxers?"

"I've seen 'em," Willie said.

"Is there anything you haven't branded?"

"I don't know. I lose track every now and then."

"Think it's time to get going, boys," Phil said in a way that wasn't a question.

Hunter stared out into the dark countryside. This might be the last memory like this he ever had. Right before the crazy hunters from the Louisiana backwoods took him out and killed him. He'd seen shows about crazy killers from Louisiana.

"Ready to become a man?" Willie asked him.

"There are lots of responses I could say to that," Hunter said.

Willie was already climbing onto a four-wheeler. "Keep 'em to yourself!"

They were off, into the pit of the early morning shadows.

Once again Hunter wondered what in the world he was doing there.

10

IT CAME UPON a DUCK BLIND SO CLEAR

Sometime between getting on the four-wheeler and getting off by the swamp, Hunter got a nice, cold splash of mud streaked across his face.

"There you go," Willie said as he was driving. "You don't need any camo on your face."

It was a sign of things to come. Bad things. Things that made him miss his warm house and his comfortable sofa and his video games and his iPhone and everything else.

When he met Willie's brother Jase and uncle Si, both of them acted about as enthusiastic as Hunter did. They barely managed a "Hey there" before talking about their business. The group followed Phil into the swamp. The land they happened to be hunting on was the Robertsons'. Hunter found it kinda crazy that Phil could be living in a modest little house and yet seem to own acres of property. Maybe that's the way he liked it. Maybe he really just wanted to live out here in the wilderness like a wild man in prehistoric times.

There was a new term Hunter discovered. One of many: *waders*. These were the waterproof pant/boot outfits they were all wearing. Actually they were called chest waders, but Hunter didn't really take that much notice. He doubted he would ever need to know what chest waders were after this day.

But good thing I got some really awesome snow camo that I bought for myself.

It took about ten minutes before Hunter realized his waders were leaking.

"I think I'm getting a little wet," he said.

John Luke just glanced at him and said nothing. Jase was leading the pack along with his father,

Phil. Uncle Si was talking about something. Willie was the only one who responded.

"Well, son, that's generally what happens when you go hunting."

"What?"

"You get wet. And muddy. And sore. And stinky. Sometimes every muscle in your body will ache. Sometimes you start to hyperventilate. Sometimes you black out."

"Really?"

Willie laughed. "Nah. Not usually. But this is all part of the fun."

"Fun?"

"I know one thing, Hunter. You'll never forget this."

His feet felt cold and squishy.

"Yeah, you're right about that."

Hunter could think of lots of things it would have been nice to know before heading into swampland with the bearded rednecks.

Like the dog, for instance. Hunter didn't know it was a bad thing to insult a duck dog.

When Hunter first saw the black Lab walking with them in the swamp, he jumped. He hadn't seen the dog before and thought it might be some kind of wild animal or something. Obviously the guys knew the black Lab.

"What's his name?" Hunter asked Phil, who had slowed down to be by the dog.

"*Her* name. This is Peggy Sue."

Hunter reached down and petted the dog. But instead of showing any affection toward him, she ignored him completely.

"Ooh. Guess Peggy's never met a hunter from Chicago. Come on, girl."

Peggy Sue looked like an older dog and seemed to struggle walking through the thick swamp.

"Can she even find the ducks you shoot down?"

Phil looked back at Hunter but didn't say anything. Even in the darkness Phil was wearing his sunglasses.

Does he ever take those things off?

Maybe he was like a superhero. Maybe the sunglasses were like Batman's mask or Superman's cape.

A few moments later, Willie tugged at Hunter's arm and stopped him.

"What's up?" Hunter asked.

"Just a little tip. Never make fun of a man's dog. That's almost as bad as making fun of his wife. Sometimes worse."

"I was just saying she looks kinda old."

"Uncle Si looks old too. Doesn't mean he can't hunt. Even if he does hunt with a 28-gauge."

At this point, Hunter didn't know if what was being directed at him was real or humor. He simply decided to be quiet for a while and not say anything. Especially about the dog that obviously didn't take a liking to him.

Willie said there were probably around forty duck blinds on their property. But they were all heading to a particular one.

The one farthest away from civilization.

They had almost arrived when Hunter slipped on something and then *BOOM*. His shotgun went off.

Thankfully John Luke was no longer walking left of him.

Hunter looked at the shotgun as if it were alive.

"Hey, Chicago," Phil said, "didn't I tell you to make sure the safety was on?"

"I thought it was on!"

"I don't think it was."

"I think he might've blasted a frog to bits," Jase joked.

"I think he blasted my eardrums to bits," Uncle Si said.

"I'm sorry."

"*Sorry*s are nice until you're having to say it to the mother of the son you just shot." Phil's words were just like any of the others he said. Blunt and direct and without emotion.

"The safety is on."

Hunter felt like a bigger moron now. A muddy, cold, and wet moron.

Hearing the guys talking in the duck blind made Hunter think of Carson. It made him consider all the things he had missed and was going to miss not being around his brother. When his parents decided to get a divorce, it didn't just mean that they wouldn't be together. It meant he and Carson wouldn't be together, either. That had been the toughest thing.

No, seeing Carson not care a bit was the toughest thing.

Willie and Jase seemed to enjoy going back and forth on things. Jase would complain and Willie would make fun of him and then Jase would make Willie out to be a crazy, lazy person. Phil said little. Uncle Si said things every now and then, but Hunter couldn't make any sense of them.

The sun began creeping up over the tops of the large trees in the swamp. They were sitting, looking at the sky. So far duck hunting was definitely not Hunter's thing.

"So, Chicago, what would you being doing back at home?" Phil said.

"He'd be sleeping," Willie said. "Most people would."

"Yeah," Hunter agreed.

Conversation continued, and they eventually asked Hunter if he'd truly never been hunting before.

"I've been to the Brookfield Zoo around Chicago."

"But you've never shot at any kind of animal?" Jase asked. "No squirrel hunting of any kind?"

"I think we'd be arrested shooting anything around where we live. We don't have property to hunt on like this. But once there was a coyote that came in our backyard. And the thing was huge. It was scary, too—"

Phil said something, but Hunter didn't really hear him. As he kept talking, Hunter looked up at the sky that was getting brighter by the second. But he didn't really pay attention to what he was looking at.

"We have a shih tzu and it was outside and my mom almost freaked out because that coyote would have—"

"Shh," Willie said, nudging him.

They were squatting on the duck blind and, out of the corner of his eye, Hunter spotted some ducks flying past. But too late.

"They're gone," Jase said.

"Think they heard Capone here talking about his puppy," Phil said.

"Sorry."

"When we see ducks, we get quiet."

It was as if the ducks told all the other ducks not to go past this site. The next few minutes or hours or days (it all seemed like an eternity to Hunter), they were sitting there in the duck blind, staring at the sky and blowing the duck call. Soon Hunter began to hear those sounds in his brain. It was all he could hear and nothing else. He would be hearing duck calls for the rest of his life.

Quack, quack, quack. Echoes of the duck in his mind and body and soul.

"Think they'll be coming?" Jase asked.

"Oh, I think they'll be coming," Phil said.

At the first sign of the ducks, Phil said something Hunter didn't understand.

"Cut 'em, boys," he said like a general to his troops.

Everybody stood and took shots. Everybody except Hunter.

They took down a few and then argued over who shot which one.

"When he says 'cut 'em,' that means stand and shoot," Willie said.

Hunter nodded.

I'd feel so much better if I was at a Thirty Seconds to Mars concert. At least I'd know what to do there.

It was amazing to see Peggy Sue swimming to find the ducks. With morning fully there now, Hunter could watch things. He could see how the men blew their duck calls and somehow maneuvered their lips and hands in a way he'd never be able to. Ever. He could see how their eyes never left the sky. He noticed how they were ready for the right moment when—

"Get ready, Phil," Uncle Si said as a group of ducks appeared in the distance.

Now was the time to show his manhood.

Don't blow it.

He'd show them. Chicago Hunter or Capone or Da Bears or whatever else they called him was going to show them.

Hunter stood and fired off a blast. Then another. Then another.

The ducks flew away.

"Way too far away," Willie said.

"I think Capone there just scared off the rest of the ducks for the day," Phil said.

"Sorry."

"We already had a discussion about that word, didn't we?" Phil asked him.

"Yeah."

"That, son, is called skybusting," Willie said.

Hunter just nodded. *I tried to bust open the sky or something?*

"It's when you shoot out of range," Willie continued. "They have to be thirty-five yards or closer."

Phil looked at Hunter. "If you can see the eye, the bird will die."

Everybody had already shot several ducks. Well, everybody except Hunter. It seemed like they were waiting on him to kill at least one. But the sun was getting bigger and the sky was getting brighter and he actually started to feel a bit warm.

It's not gonna happen.

"Hunter." Willie was sitting behind him, no longer looking up but staring at him.

"Yeah."

"How many times have you fired that shotgun? Well, not including the time you shot a poor, defenseless tree in the dark."

"A dozen? Maybe more."

"So you figure it's time to give up?"

Hunter wasn't sure if this was a trick question or what. "I don't know."

"Yeah, you do. You tell me. Think it's time to call it a morning and head back?"

Hunter looked at the others, but nobody was

saying a word. "I'd really like to kill at least one. To say I did."

"Okay, then. That's what's gonna happen."

"You know—it could take a long time before we see any more ducks," Jase said.

"Don't listen to him," Willie said. "He's a born pessimist. You gotta think big."

Fifteen minutes later, Phil was the one to say, "Cut 'em." And Hunter was the only one who stood this time, firing off five shots.

Right after, Hunter felt a clap on his shoulder.

"See what you did?" Willie said.

"Did I get one?"

"You got two!" Uncle Si shouted. "Those were good shots for anybody."

"Capone finally lives up to his name," Phil said.

Hunter wasn't sure, but he thought he might have seen a smile on Phil's face.

As they walked back to the four-wheeler twenty minutes later, Hunter brought up the rear with Phil.

"So you killed your first duck," Phil said in a proud way. "How's it feel?"

Clouds covered the sky in all directions, but Hunter felt as though he could see slivers of light.

"Feels pretty good," he said.

"You know what I call it?"

"What?"

"I'd say it feels pretty happy, happy, happy."

Hunter laughed. He'd seen something in John Luke's room with that saying on it and had no idea where it came from.

"And you know what Genesis says?" Phil continued. "'Everything that lives and moves about will be food for you.' Those ducks will be tasty."

Hunter was beginning to realize preaching and Bible quoting were part of Phil's normal speech.

Then he thought of something else and decided to just go ahead and say it. "I wish Carson could've been here."

"Who's that?"

"My older brother. He lives with my dad."

"I reckon you don't live with them?"

"No."

"Ah," Phil said with a nod. "Well, you tell him as soon as you can what you did. You send him the picture John Luke took of you."

"Yeah."

"Brothers are a special thing. I have four of them. Si is a couple of years younger than me, so we've always been pretty tight."

"I don't think Carson and me will ever be tight."

"You never know," Phil said. "You live as long as I have and you can say you've seen lots of things happen. Life's one grand mystery that's never fully gonna be solved. But you can have fun trying."

11
WHAT CRAZY CHILD IS THIS?

Hunter stared at the dining table and the kitchen just behind it. Sitting on the sofa in Phil and Kay's home, he felt a bit smothered by the thousands of Christmas decorations and collectibles and items that were everywhere.

Everywhere.

As you walked into the small house, garland edged the walls, which were filled with dozens of Christmas cards. It looked like there were maybe five hundred Christmas cards in various places. Hunter wondered if these were all cards they got this year. Hunter and his mother might be fortunate if they got a half dozen themselves. And Mom never decorated the house. He'd be lucky if she finished decorating their fake Christmas tree that seemed to get a little smaller each season.

"So how'd it go?" Miss Kay called out from behind the stove.

The smells from the kitchen were making him even hungrier than he already was. Hunter shrugged and told Miss Kay that it was fine. They were the only ones in the house since Phil had asked the guys to help him with something out back.

"Well, it sure doesn't look fine by your sad face," Miss Kay said, watching him with friendly eyes. "Come on in here for a minute."

The light granite top of the long, rectangular island in the center of the kitchen held a variety of bowls and cooking utensils and wooden chopping blocks with knives on them. It looked like a dozen of Santa's little helpers had been in there helping Miss Kay with her Christmas meal. A couple pots were on burners cooking something. A fresh pan of biscuits cooled beside the oven.

For a family that was supposed to be so rich and famous, this kitchen was only as big as the one in Hunter's own house. And it was smaller than the one at his father's house, though that was for show. Dad didn't know what the word *cook* actually meant unless it was someone who was paid to do it right there in front of you.

"So did you survive going into the wilderness with the wild Robertson men?" Miss Kay asked.

"Yeah." *Just glad I didn't accidentally kill one of the Robertsons.*

"They weren't too mean to you, were they?"

"No, it was cool," Hunter said. *Of course I might never go hunting again in my entire life.* But deep down, he hoped he would.

Steam was rising from a pot. Miss Kay had batter or something white on her cheek. She gave him a friendly grin. "You know Phil's just a big teddy bear."

Hunter thought of how he looked late last night standing at the edge of the family room.

Yeah, a pretty scary teddy bear.

"There was a time in our lives he wasn't so nice," Miss Kay said. "But he was running from everybody, mostly God. Sometimes you gotta run a long ways off before you're finally found."

She put a twelve-inch loaf of French bread on a cookie sheet in front of him. "So last night I taught you how to make carrot cake. That wasn't so painful, was it?"

"No. Actually it was pretty good."

"See—maybe I'll make a chef out of you. Forget the hunting and the fishing. You do know the Robertson men are wonderful cooks, right?"

Hunter was surprised to hear this. "No, I didn't know that. They don't leave the cooking to the ladies?"

"Not at all. One might think so, but they love making meals. They love eatin' 'em too. So here— this thing of French bread. I'm going to teach you how to bake something and how to become Willie's best friend forever."

"Bread?" Hunter asked.

"Oh no. This isn't just any kind of bread. This is Willie's crazy bread."

"What's so crazy about it?"

"It's crazy good. In a Robertson kind of way."

Something about the way Miss Kay said that in her Southern accent made Hunter feel a bit more comfortable. A bit less like he needed to sprint out of this kitchen and through the door and into the surrounding woods. He doubted he'd ever be completely at home here, but at least he was able to breathe a bit easier.

"Surely you've cooked a little in your life?" Miss Kay asked.

"Uh . . . I took cooking classes the same time I took duck hunting lessons."

For a second, she nodded before looking him in the eyes and laughing. "You're funny."

"I struggle to make Campbell's soup."

"Well, this is simple and memorable. First, get yourself a nice loaf of bread like this. Heat the oven to four hundred degrees. Then start cutting the bread like this—about an inch apart or so. Here, I'll let you do it. But don't cut all the way through."

Hunter carefully worked the knife into the bread.

"It's not gonna break or blow up," she said. "Keep going."

She brought over a dish with some kind of liquid in it. "This is melted butter. You want a stick of this. Melt it on top of the stove. Now pour this between the slices. Go ahead, slowly. Make sure you have enough to go around."

Hunter finished that and then was given a cup of mozzarella cheese. He felt awkward doing anything in the kitchen, but Miss Kay couldn't have been more patient or kind with him as he did what he was told.

"Now just a teaspoon of garlic salt," Miss Kay said. "I'll do this. You get those bacon slices over there and start putting them on top of each piece of bread."

This was easy enough to do. Once finished, Miss Kay told him that was it.

"We cook it until the cheese melts; then we

change the oven over to broil so the bacon can bake. And there you have it. Willie's crazy bread."

The door opened and the guys were walking in.

"Shhh," Miss Kay said. "Go ahead—put it in the oven."

Hunter slipped the pan inside while the guys took off their coats and came around the kitchen island.

"What's up, guys?" Willie said.

"I'm teaching Hunter here some easy recipes," Miss Kay said.

Willie placed a hand over his stomach. "What's for lunch?"

"A surprise," Miss Kay said. "I have a few more things to show our guest."

"Is this leftover spinach dip?"

"I just warmed that up."

Willie took a cracker and scooped up a fistful of dip. With a full mouth he moaned, "This is the best. You gotta try some of it."

"I don't like spinach," Hunter said.

"Uh-uh," Willie said after he swallowed and

could talk again. "This isn't spinach. It's like a little bit of heaven dripped down and got mixed in this bowl with some spinach."

"I think you're referring to the butter and cream cheese and sour cream," Miss Kay said.

"Heaven. That's what heaven's gonna be. Rivers of cream cheese and sour cream. All you can eat."

Uncle Si meandered into the kitchen and spotted the biscuits. He was about to grab one when Miss Kay noticed and forced him and Willie out.

"We'll be eating in just a minute. Now y'all go on. I'm going to try to give this Yankee as much help as he can get before he leaves Louisiana."

I need a lot of help. More than you could possibly know.

The prayer surprised him.

Maybe people around these parts were familiar with sitting around a table and pausing for a moment to pray. But Hunter wasn't one of those.

He had a mouth full of bread when Phil told them they were going to offer the blessing for the meal.

He'd already heard a few prayers before the meals, but there was something about this one that moved Hunter. Maybe because the blessing went beyond the food.

"Lord, thank you for all the bountiful blessings you provide, and thank you for the gift of your Son and our Savior, Jesus Christ. We thank you for bringing Hunter down here to spend Christmas with us. Lord, bless our time with him and help him to know he can relax around us. Unless it's two in the morning and he's playing the television too loud. In your Son's name, amen."

When Hunter looked up, Phil wasn't grinning or looking to see if he'd been clever with his comments. No, they were getting busy dishing up the food.

"Thank you for bringing Hunter down here . . ."

He wasn't sure what to think about this. Food was one thing, and sitting there at the table was another, but being thanked for coming by? That was crazy.

This whole Christmas was crazy. It was like the type of dream you had whenever you experienced a bad fever. Soon he'd wake up and the redneck dreams would be over and life would be back to its quiet and calm normalcy.

"Hunter, would you like to share what you made for the boys?"

He brought out Willie's crazy bread, and instantly the room seemed to erupt in applause and hysteria. Like someone scored the winning touchdown in a football game.

"Hunter, you have just become my best friend," Willie said. He truly looked happy. Like a kid on Christmas.

And as Hunter stood there, feeling a bit embarrassed and also a bit proud of what he'd done, he had the strangest feeling.

For some crazy, wacky reason, he suddenly didn't want to go back home.

12
MAYBE THEY DON'T KNOW IT'S CHRISTMAS

"I picked up a few more paper angels for us to get presents for."

The SUV was parked in a very busy parking lot in front of Target. Korie gave each of the kids a slip of paper that had a name and other assorted details on it. Hunter was sitting in the passenger seat next to her and obviously didn't know what she was talking about.

"Okay, I'll explain this. Have you ever heard of the Angel Tree program?"

"No," Hunter said. "But I know that the teacher says every time a bell rings, an angel gets his wings."

Everyone burst out laughing.

"That was funny," Sadie said from the backseat. "Like clever funny."

This prompted lots of color on Hunter's face.

"Well, they have these trees around—I'm sure you've seen them in shopping malls or something— and they have names on them. They're kids who won't be getting presents for Christmas for one reason or another. Usually poor kids whose parents can't afford to get them anything. So on this form are the items they want. What name do you have?"

"Uh, Marlo. She's three."

"Oh, great. There's a girl named Marlo who you'll be buying for."

Hunter looked uncomfortable. "What do I get for a three-year-old?"

"Whatever's on the list."

He started reading some of the items. "'Fisher-Price Little People, Barbie, a bike'?"

"See—you have lots to pick from," Korie said. "We've done this every year. Our church has a tree they put up. We had already gotten some names but I figured since you were here, we could get some more."

Hunter thought about how much money he had. *Doesn't matter. It's probably a good thing to do.*

"Don't worry—this is always a lot of fun. And we've helped hand out the gifts at church in years past."

Soon Hunter was following the five siblings toward the store.

It was nice to have showered and changed clothes back at the Robertsons' house this afternoon. He almost felt like himself again. He was no longer freezing and wet. His belly did feel a little tight, but he knew that was for obvious reasons.

That crazy bread sure was awesome.

"You need help there?" Sadie asked him.

"She will only make things more complicated," John Luke said.

"No, I won't. I'm the world's best shopper."

"She gets lost in stores," Will said, rolling his eyes.

Hunter couldn't imagine Korie as a young mother dealing with all these kids. Dealing with even a couple of them. He didn't want to ask her age but she must have had the children really, really young.

As they entered Target, almost every other person greeted them.

"Korie!"

"Hey, John Luke!"

"Hi, Sadie!"

For the first time since . . . well, maybe the first time ever, Hunter realized the Robertsons really were well-known.

People were giving him looks, wondering who he was.

Yeah, I'm Sadie's boyfriend. That's right. No pictures please—don't let this show up on Instagram.

He actually felt sorta dumb following the Robertsons, not really being part of their family.

"Come on, Hunter," Korie called out to him as if she could read his mind.

They were heading through the store. Through the chaos of the shopping vortex just a couple of days before Christmas.

He stared at the paper angel in his hand. *So,*

Marlo. What kind of presents can I get you to make your mommy and daddy proud?

Hunter hoped he'd find the right sort of presents. He was going to try his best.

When they reached the checkout line and Hunter tried to pay for his items, Korie laughed.

"No, no, we have this," she told him. "I didn't expect you to pay."

"It's okay."

"No, this is our treat. I just wanted you to get the chance to pick out the items. What'd you get?"

Hunter showed her the items in his shopping cart. He'd chosen a pink bunny, a couple of Fisher-Price Little People toy sets, and a pink tricycle.

"Nice bike," Korie said.

"It's a 'Radio Flyer Classic Pink Dual Deck Tricycle,'" Hunter read off the label. "Definitely looks like a girl's bike."

"I think John Luke used to have one just like it," Rebecca joked.

"Excellent selections," Korie said. "We'll bring them to the church later on."

It never dawned on Hunter that there were kids who didn't get Christmas presents every year. He knew there were poor families out there, but he hadn't thought much about what they did for Christmas.

"So these will get to them by Christmas?"

"These were kids whose names hadn't been picked. The church made one last announcement to hopefully get all the angels picked. So yeah— the presents get to them by Christmas morning."

"Cool."

On the way back home, John Luke sat in the passenger's seat while Hunter sat in the back with the rest of the kids.

"So, Hunter, what's your story?" Rebecca asked him.

She sat next to him in the SUV, and he felt like a fool around her and Sadie. He just shrugged and said nothing.

"You don't look as freaked out as you did yesterday," Rebecca said. "That's impressive. I was sixteen when I came to live with the Robertsons, and I was so overwhelmed that I hardly left my room for two weeks."

He imagined lots of different replies, but none of them seemed right.

"Anyway, what do you do in Chicago?" she asked.

"I live in a suburb, not really Chicago," Hunter said.

"What do you do in that suburb?"

He shrugged. "I don't know—normal things."

"Like?"

They were all waiting on him to say something and he felt like a complete doofus sitting there.

What do you like to do, Hunter? Play video games? Sleep? Watch television?

Rebecca designed clothing. At least that's what Hunter thought he'd heard. She looked very fashionable, so he could see her doing that.

He looked very ordinary.

"I don't know," he said. That was it.

Boring. Lame-o Hunter.

It wasn't long before everybody started talking about something else. Conversation among the Robertsons never seemed awkward. But Hunter was a walking billboard for awkwardness.

He kept replaying his words in his mind. *"I don't know."*

They were probably all so disappointed that he hadn't turned out to be someone far cooler or more interesting or more *anything* than he really was.

"Hello, this is Hunter, and he's still not sure who he is."

That's what any of them could say if introducing him to the rest of the world.

Some people in this life deserved to have the bright lights shone on them. Others, like Hunter, were the ones in the background. No one aiming the lights at them.

No. He was the one tripping over the electrical cord.

Yeah.

13
DING DONG DUCK MERRILY on HIGH

Korie had started to prepare the meal when Hunter wandered into the kitchen, looking bored and lost. It was perfect timing—she'd been about to go get him.

"What's going on?"

Hunter shrugged. Ever since the car ride home, the kid had been more quiet. Since coming inside, he'd resorted to being indifferent and a bit sulky. Will had asked a couple of times if he wanted to play a video game but Hunter said no. He'd been glued to his iPhone, sitting and staring at it and remaining silent.

"Miss Kay said she taught you a few recipes."

Again, the casual and distant nod.

"Want to learn how to make duck and dressing? I thought you might be interested."

"Duck?"

Korie never stopped moving but kept talking to Hunter. "Yeah, the ducks y'all killed this morning."

"Gross."

"What's gross about that?"

"Will I have to spit out the shotgun pellets?"

She shook her head and laughed. "No, I wouldn't worry about that. Come on—I thought you needed to have a little duck and dressing." Her tone became confidential. "This might surprise you, but Willie's the real cook around here, not me. Phil's good too. Phil showed me how to make duck and dressing one time, but I never thought I'd have to do it myself. I wanted to give it a try today, just for you."

"You know the dinner in *Christmas Vacation*? That's the kind of turkey my mom makes."

She wanted to ask Hunter if he could think of one—just one—positive thought for the moment.

"I already have the ducks in a large pot. I have three teals in there."

"Teals?"

"Those are types of ducks."

"Oh."

"Don't worry. You'll learn soon enough."

"Duck knowledge sure will get me far in Illinois," Hunter said in a smug, sarcastic way.

"It got Phil pretty far," Korie said.

"Is duck all you guys eat?" Hunter asked.

She chose not to answer that question but kept chatting. "You know, when John Luke was younger, he was such an animal lover, so we were a little worried about him and hunting. His grandfather and father made a living out of hunting, you know? We weren't sure what was going to happen. But you know that massive elk in the other room? The one on the wall?"

Hunter nodded.

"John Luke was eleven years old when he shot that. It was the first thing he ever got. He and Willie went on a ten-day hunt, and John Luke came back with that massive elk. So the first meal we had, we made a big deal about John Luke providing the dinner for that night. All that winter, we ate from that elk. Elk roast, everything. And John Luke was proud of it. He understood why people hunt."

"You guys aren't gonna make me eat the heart of a duck or anything like that?"

"No. Well, I won't. But I can never speak for Willie." Korie smiled. "Now, let's get going. This is a learning experience for me too, so we'll figure it out together."

For the next half hour, she went over how to make one of Phil's favorite recipes. "The ducks will have to cook for a little under two hours. But he says that makes the meal so much better."

She went through each step on how to make the dressing. And with each passing minute, it somehow seemed like Hunter was actually listening and trying to learn. That he *wanted* to learn. The distant, disconnected kid started to go away. In his place was someone genuinely curious. Like the oven in the kitchen, Hunter was warming up.

"So you mix everything together with your hands?" he asked about the dressing.

"Sure—go ahead."

Hunter's hands slowly combined the corn bread, saltines, Ritz crackers, and white bread together.

"You're doing fine," Korie encouraged.

Near the end it was obvious that Hunter liked seeing something accomplished.

"You say you don't like cooking back home?" she asked him.

"I never do any of it, so I don't know."

"You might find you like it more than you'd think."

Hunter wiped his wet hands on a towel. "Well, I'd be making meals for one."

As Korie tried to think of a proper response to his statement, Sadie walked into the kitchen and began talking. Hunter started to slip out toward the family room.

"Thank you, Hunter," Korie called before he left the room.

"Sure."

Before dinner, Korie pulled John Luke away from the rest of the kids to talk with him for a minute.

"What are you doing tonight?"

"I don't know," John Luke said. "Maybe going to see a movie with some of the guys."

"Can you bring Hunter?"

A lot of kids might have made a face and asked their mother to give them a break. But John Luke simply nodded and said, "Sure."

"And make sure he doesn't check out," Korie said.

"I can't help if he does that."

"I know. But just . . . be aware that it could happen."

"Okay."

She wanted to say more, but this time she held back, not because she didn't have the words to say but rather because it wasn't the right time.

"What's wrong?" John Luke asked.

"Nothing. Not one thing."

She didn't want to tell him how much it was going to hurt to see him head off to college. She wasn't about to go there and get all melancholy and sad. That wasn't like her.

Then again, your firstborn only leaves home once.

When she finally got ahold of Willie after calling several times, he was acting strange again.

"What have you been up to?" she asked. "I have dinner almost ready."

"Oh, just busy doing stuff."

She knew what the vagueness meant. He was doing something very specific and he very much didn't want to tell her about it.

"Willie Jess Robertson, what are you hiding from me?"

He laughed into the phone. "Okay, you got me. I've been planning this amazing gift for you that's taking hours and hours to create."

If there's one thing that Willie didn't do, it was

take hours and hours to do anything. He just didn't have that much time available.

"Now I know you're lying."

"Are you really making a big dinner tonight?"

"Duck and dressing," Korie said. "Just like I told you I was going to."

"You sure Phil isn't in the kitchen somewhere?"

"Hunter and I are fully capable. Prepare to be amazed."

He laughed. "Okay, great. Hey, I got an idea."

"An idea for what?"

"You know Mrs. Wallace from church?"

"Yeah."

"Well, her husband is officially gone. Just like that."

"What?"

"Yeah," Willie said. "Two days before Christmas."

"Oh no. She's got young kids."

"Uh-huh. So here's my idea."

Korie listened, and as much as she didn't want to change her plans for dinner, as hard as she and

Hunter had worked on the meal, she also knew Willie's idea was the right thing to do.

"So are you coming home, then?" Korie asked.

"Right now."

"Hunter's going to be disappointed. Actually, *I'm* going to be disappointed."

"That's part of life. Part of growing up, right? This'll be a valuable life lesson for good ole Hunter."

"Something tells me he doesn't want to be in school. Especially with Professor Willie."

"Hey, I like the ring of that. See you soon."

For a moment Korie thought of telling Hunter, but then she decided that could be Willie's job. It was his wonderful idea in the first place. She didn't want to rob her husband the pleasure of really, truly ruining Hunter's evening.

14
HERE COMES WILLIE CLAUS

Hunter was furious.

First Willie had come home carrying Subway sandwiches. *Subway* sandwiches. All the work he'd done in the kitchen preparing dinner was now out the window. Willie just walked in and told Hunter that plans change.

"We're gonna be taking the dinner to someone tonight."

That was all he had said before disappearing to his office or bedroom or man cave. Hunter had wanted to say many things to him.

Uh, excuse me, but did you make this meal, mister?

Hey, dude, I can get Subway back home.

I helped kill them. I helped cook them. Now I wanna help eat them.

Instead Hunter remained silent, playing Candy Crush on his iPhone.

"I'm sorry, Hunter," Korie said. "There's a family at church who . . ."

Hunter didn't listen to the rest of what Korie said. He didn't want to or need to. Yeah, yeah, yeah. He got it. Family in need. But couldn't the family in need get the Subway? Did they *have* to have the duck and dressing? Seriously?

When everybody gathered around the table to eat their sandwiches, Hunter said he wasn't hungry.

"Oh, come on. Teenage boys are *always* hungry."

But he just stayed on the couch. Quiet. Angry.

After dinner, while they were cleaning up and talking and laughing, Willie grabbed his car keys. "I think Hunter's gonna come with me to deliver this wonderful meal. He can take all the credit in the world for making it."

"I can stay here," Hunter said.

Willie laughed. "Hey, Hunter. Get up. You're coming with me. Now."

The tone told him enough.

Get up, Hunter.

So he did.

They climbed into a camouflage-patterned BMW roadster. It was the first time Hunter had seen it.

"Wow—cool car."

"Yeah. *Nobody* knows who I am when I drive this." He nudged Hunter with an elbow.

Soon Willie was racing around the corners and making Hunter carefully hold the dishes at his feet.

"So, Hunter. Let me tell you a few things that will help you when you get older. First off, do you know the most important job out there in the world today?"

"Being a duck commander?" Hunter said in a dry tone.

Willie just chuckled. "Now I'm assuming you're trying to be funny. Actually, that's number two. No, the number one job is being a mother. You know that, right? You have a mother."

"I don't think she got the memo."

"Well, maybe not. But it is. And one of the toughest times for any mother—any parent, really, but fathers got it made—is when the kids are two and three years old. The toddler stage. These are brutal times for a mother. You understand?"

"Yeah."

"No, listen. I'm being serious. *Brutal.* So look here. There's a family at our church that's been going through some rough times. I think you can appreciate this because you've been through them. The parents have been separated and trying to work through things. But today I got informed that the father split on his family. Literally took off. Boom. Just like that. Left a mother with a three-year-old and an eighteen-month-old. A son and a daughter."

Hunter watched the passing countryside but didn't say anything.

"This made me think of John Luke and Sadie. How hard having kids that age already was. And then being left *alone*? Two days before Christmas? That's crazy, huh?"

"Yeah."

"So what's the easiest thing we could do?"

"Bring some food over there?" Hunter answered.

"Yes, sir. And I'll just try to ignore that wonderful tone of yours."

Hunter was still irritated. He didn't understand why it had to be *this* particular meal.

"There are times when I get tired of people asking me for things," Willie said. "Once things got big—really big—for Duck Commander, I realized I had about ten times the relatives and friends out there. And sometimes that drives me crazy."

The BMW curled around a curve at a crazy speed.

"But then I have to step back and be reminded that everything I have—*every single thing*—is a gift from God. Doesn't mean I have to give it all away. But gifts are just that; they are things that you don't ask for but someone gives to you. This—this is nothing. This is just to help Mrs. Wallace and her kids in the here and now. But you know, it's not an easy road ahead, is it?"

"No."

Hunter looked away from him, out the window. He didn't want to admit it, but he was starting to feel a little guilty.

It was one thing to hear Willie Robertson talking about giving gifts and being good and Christmas. But it was another thing to see the mother and her kids.

They weren't living in some run-down trailer in the middle of honky-tonk land. No. She was in a modest, one-story house. She appeared at the door with a frazzled and completely baffled look on her face.

"Willie, what are you doing here?" she asked. She talked to him like they could have been classmates.

Maybe they were.

"Well, I have a special guest staying with us who

is turning out to be something of a chef. Right, Hunter? Hunter, this is Judy Wallace."

Hunter nodded since he was carrying a dish in his hands.

"Come on in, please," Mrs. Wallace said.

Inside, the kids were tiny terrors. Loud, whining, and all over the place.

"Please tell me you didn't have dinner yet," Willie said to the woman.

"I barely had lunch."

She wore black sweatpants and a T-shirt. Her hair was in a ponytail and she wasn't wearing any makeup. She was pretty but also seemed very tough and no-nonsense.

"We just wanted to bring you some duck and dressing. Hunter helped kill the ducks this morning and then cook them."

"First time," Hunter added.

That was when Mrs. Wallace broke down and started crying. Willie went over and gave her a hug and said, "Now, now, I know it can't taste *that* bad."

Hunter felt awkward enough to pass out, so

it was such a relief to have some humor thrown
in there.

"We're just thinking about you, okay? Not only
the Robertsons but the church. Anything we can do,
you let us know. Okay?" Willie gave her an envelope
that looked like it might hold a Christmas card.

Hunter wondered if there was something else
inside that card. Something to help Mrs. Wallace.

A boy came in asking for some chips while the
little girl was tugging at her leg.

"It's always crazy like this," Mrs. Wallace said.

"Yeah. I remember those days. I'm not sure I'd
want to relive them for long."

They talked for a little while, but Willie made
it clear he didn't want to disturb her. He just said
again they'd be praying for her and left things at
that. She hugged both of them before they left.

Back in the car, Willie started it up and looked
at Hunter. "Still want your duck and dressing?"
he asked.

"No."

"You know what's cool about this?" Willie said.

"It's a bunch of firsts here. Your first hunt. Your first kill. Your first cooking experience. All while Mrs. Wallace is going through a bunch of firsts herself. Not the best kind, of course. But it's nice to combat the bad firsts with the good ones. You know?"

"Yeah."

"And, Hunter—after all the food you're going to eat in the next two days, trust me. You'll *thank* me."

Hunter almost thanked him for giving him so much credit with the duck and the meal, but he didn't.

It would have been another first. Thanking someone spontaneously.

Hunter didn't want to have too much of a good thing. So he let it go.

15

SILENT NIGHT
at the ROBERTSONS'

Sometimes it just took a fleeting, solitary moment
to make her stop and realize all she had to be
thankful for.

Maybe it was the news about the Wallaces.
Maybe it was having Hunter staying with them.
Maybe it was because this was John Luke's last
Christmas with them before college.

Maybe it was all of that and more. Korie wasn't
sure.

But with the younger kids watching television
in the other room and Willie somewhere doing

something and Sadie hanging out with her boyfriend and John Luke taking Hunter out with friends, she found herself alone. Actually able to tweet a fun picture she took of the kids earlier. Actually able to sip some tea and stare at the Nativity set on the counter.

She always got to a point every Christmas where she would tell Willie that next year they would spend the holiday in the Bahamas. But she knew she could never do such a thing. It just wouldn't be the same without having all her family around her. Without the traditions and the laughter and the familiar smiles and the familiar joy.

Thank you, Lord, for the familiar things we so often forget.

It was easy to carry her thankfulness around like a credit card in her purse. Every now and then it could be taken out and viewed and charged, but all too often it got stuck in the dark in the middle of lots of other items. Unused. Unthought of. Untouched.

She went over to a wall full of family photos—

visual reminders of all the things she was grateful for. Her parents, who were never too far away and were still important parts of her personal and professional life. Their parents and the amazing heritage of faith they had passed on to her family from both sides. Both grandparents were great examples of men and women faithful to God and to their marriages. Both sides had their share of difficulties throughout their lives but never wavered in their faith. And a testimony to that could now be seen on Sunday mornings when their family took up three rows at church.

The smiling faces revealed so much about life to her. She was grateful for Willie always thinking and dreaming big. She loved John Luke's adventurous heart. Sadie's ability to make life fun. Will's sweet hugs. The way Bella made those around her smile. Rebecca's fun spirit.

Thank you, Lord, for all these smiles and for the stored-away memories each of them brings.

Maybe there would be a season in her life when she was older and she was left with those memories

A ROBERTSON FAMILY CHRISTMAS

to pass the time. She'd be feeding chicken soup to Willie at a retirement home and she'd recount all the good times they'd had. The busy days and the blurry nights. The exhausted moments.

Lots of love and laughter surrounded them. And by God's grace, that's how they made it through.

Thank you for those moments and for this moment.

Korie thought of Hunter and prayed for him. That his heart would open up a little more and that they could be as much of a family to him as he wanted them to be. She asked for help because she knew they certainly could use it.

Then she thanked God for the whole reason around this mad rush of a holiday. The reason they celebrated Christmas: Jesus' birth into this fallen world.

It was good to keep the focus on the why.

16
DO YOU HEAR THAT AWFUL SONG I HEAR?

That night, after going to see a movie with John Luke and some of his friends, Hunter almost managed to cut off John Luke's hand in a single instant.

Granted, it was John Luke's fault. But still. The Robertson family really wouldn't have liked Hunter sending John Luke to the hospital.

They went out to see the final Hobbit movie and were coming back late (since the movie was about ten hours). Hunter loved the Lord of the Rings movies and really liked the Hobbit films, but man, they felt long.

John Luke was dropping off a friend at his house, so they pulled in the driveway and the guy popped out of the car. John Luke then seemed to remember something he needed to get from his friend. He opened the door and started to climb out . . . with the Jeep still in drive.

The Jeep began to pull ahead with John Luke caught in the doorway. They had parked by another SUV, and the door was scraping along the side of the other vehicle.

Hunter freaked out and jammed the Jeep in reverse. He thought that they were going to trample the bushes along the sidewalk to the house (which they were probably doing anyway). But he didn't know exactly *why* he put the car in reverse rather than park. Now the Jeep was backing up and John Luke's arm was caught between the door and the other vehicle.

In a second, Hunter jammed the gear into park right as John Luke pulled his hand to safety. But things could have gone terribly wrong.

"Oops," John Luke simply said with a laugh. "Okay, I'll be back in a second."

Hunter took that reaction to mean John Luke might have had some other encounters with crashing his cars.

On the way back to his house, John Luke tried to make conversation, but Hunter didn't really feel much like talking. So John Luke played a song off his iPod.

"Do you like country music?"

"I'd rather be shot," Hunter said.

This made John Luke chuckle. Of course. Good times John Luke. Laid-back, everything's-gonna-be-all-right John Luke. It was unfair, really. The guy wasn't just good-looking; he was nice, too. Not fake nice or charming-before-I'm-a-total-jerk nice but genuine *nice*.

"Come on—Alan Jackson," John Luke said, blasting a song. "How can you not love this?"

The song began and it sounded like every single

country song he'd ever heard. Fast-paced with the old gee-tar playing and someone singing about a Chevy and a girl and a burger and, please, enough already.

"This is terrible."

"You've never heard this?" John Luke asked.

They were playing fiddles. Fiddles.

"No."

"It's 'Chattahoochee.' One of his best."

"Good to know in case I go on *Jeopardy!*"

There was another song he played that was a little more laid-back, but still dreadful. Still so cliché. Good times and good beer and wait, was that Spanish?

"This is the Zac Brown Band," John Luke told him.

It sounded like Jimmy Buffett, which he was *not* a fan of. But his father actually liked him a bit.

"Okay, here, I'll play you one of my favorite songs. Just listen to it."

"I can't wait."

The song started and thankfully Hunter didn't hear any fiddles or accordions or cowbells. It was a slow groove. Then he heard a familiar voice.

"John Mayer," he said. He wanted it to be clear that he knew a little about music.

John Luke nodded.

They rode in the Jeep through the dark countryside listening to John Mayer sing about gravity. And suddenly all those assorted chips on Hunter's shoulders seemed to be gone. Left behind in a Louisiana swamp.

It was good to hear a little soul spilling from the speakers.

Hunter stared out and thought about his brother. About his parents. About his family. About his life. Wondered what in the world he was doing here in the first place. Wondered why life was always causing him to come in second.

He felt goose bumps because he really wanted to believe there was some light out there in the dark. This black night felt oh-so dark and heavy and yet suddenly miles away.

Things kept pulling him down. Pulling him away. Pulling at his soul. He wanted to finally stand up and stand firm and be the guy he knew he could be. But he was a shadow in the middle of the night. Barely seen even by himself.

"You like?" John Luke asked.

"Yeah," he said.

An understatement.

But most of the things teens said came as understatements. Adults were the ones who over-did things. And he wasn't there. Not yet.

Not for a very long time.

"Love it," Hunter finally added.

The album followed them home. Few words were spoken, but the music said more than Hunter ever could.

These were cool Christmas tunes if he'd ever heard them.

Yes, sir. Gravity.

It was nice to be hovering off the ground for a moment.

He didn't want to fall back down to the hard, broken ground. Not for a while.

Keep me here a little longer. Just a little longer.

17

CHRISTMAS SWEATER TIME IS HERE

"You are not wearing that."

Korie stood in their bedroom looking in complete shock/horror/dismay/bewilderment at the outfit Willie was displaying.

"Oh, I'm wearing it," Willie said. "It's time to take the crazy Christmas sweaters up a notch."

"That is not a Christmas sweater."

He touched the fuzzy nobs that were the buttons for his shaggy, ugly Christmas *vest*. Not a sweater, but a vest.

"It doesn't have sleeves," Korie said. "And it's cut so low."

Willie lifted both of his arms and curled them like some bodybuilder. His ample chest hair spilled over Rudolph's head, giving him a fuzzy brown mane.

"Couldn't you have at least gotten a wax or something?" she joked.

"Now *that* would've been taking it up to a whole new level," Willie said. "Think there's time?"

"No. Put on one of those other sweaters."

"Bo-ring."

"Nobody wants to see all your chest hairs during Mamaw's brunch."

"I'm going to bring my comb so I can brush them," Willie said.

He wore boots and jeans and this hideous, heinous sweater vest he'd discovered somewhere. Korie's was much more cute awful with garland sticking out from it and making circles around her. It was colorful. Too colorful, in fact. Like a box of Christmas decorations had drunk too much eggnog and gotten sick and barfed all over this sweater.

Still, it was no match for Willie's.

Every Christmas Eve, her family would go over to her grandmother's house for a Christmas brunch. Most of her mother's side of the family would be there. Since there were so many family members on each side, they had to stagger the meals and the get-togethers. So this would be the first of several.

"Did you tell John Luke to give Hunter one of his sweaters?" Korie asked.

"I told him to try."

"Did you see them this morning?"

"I saw John Luke," Willie said. "Hunter was sleeping in."

"How'd it go last night?"

"I don't know. I'm assuming fine."

"I hope Hunter's getting a little more used to being here."

"They're boys," Willie said. "They don't ask each other how they feel. They grunt and fart and talk about girls."

Korie started laughing.

"What?" Willie asked.

"I can't even look at you without cracking up."

"You just can't handle my rugged masculinity."

"I can't handle all that skin. You really need to get out in the sun more."

Willie laughed. "You don't want me to try that fake tanning stuff again, do you?"

"No. You need some color. But you don't need to be orange."

Willie nodded and looked at himself in the mirror. "I'm always looking for a way to raise the bar."

She saw some fuzzy hair sticking out on his shoulder. "Oh, you're raising it all right. You might have to raise it all the way out of the dining room today."

While Andy Williams sang "It's the Most Wonderful Time of the Year" in the background, Korie felt as if she were going at the speed of the song. Fast and pulsating and bouncing and giddy. That's how it always went until the day after Christmas, when she woke up feeling like a lost, leftover marshmallow in search of her missing cup of cocoa. Right now it was the normal madness of the family shifting and coming in and out and the list of endless details slowly being whittled away.

The kids were all in the family room showing off their sweaters. They were making fun of Rebecca because hers wasn't a horrible Christmas sweater at all but actually a black-and-white comb-print sweater with a crew neck.

"I think I know where you got that from," Korie said with a smile.

"Rebecca, you're supposed to wear a crazy Christmas sweater," Sadie complained. "If I knew we could wear something from Duck & Dressing, I would have done that too."

Duck & Dressing was a boutique owned by Korie and Rebecca that offered everything from women's clothing to jewelry, handbags to home decor. The style was simple, edgy, Southern, and chic. Exactly like the sweater Rebecca wore and exactly *not* like the sweaters everybody else had on.

"It's all I have in my closet now," Rebecca protested. "This is the most festive thing I've got."

"You should've had a sweater with some duck and dressing on it," John Luke said. "That would be a better advertisement."

"Yeah, a real duck on it," Will laughed.

Korie didn't spot Hunter anywhere and asked John Luke where he might be.

"He was in my room listening to music."

"Did you tell him about the sweaters?"

John Luke nodded.

"And did you show him several he could wear?"

"I showed them to him," John Luke said.

Willie came in and the room erupted with laughter and applause. He always loved making an entrance and getting everyone's attention, especially when he could get a laugh from everybody. Once again he flexed his bare, hairy arms.

"Now *that's* what I call crazy," Sadie said.

"Rebecca, you're not allowed to wear that," Willie said.

"Yes, I can. You're crazy enough for all of us."

Korie decided to head upstairs and check on their guest.

She knocked on the door, but no one answered. As she opened it, Korie could hear muffled music. Hunter lay on the cot, his eyes closed and his head moving to the music coming from his headphones. She called his name several times and ended up tapping him on the leg. Hunter jumped a bit and looked embarrassed, turning off his music and removing the headphones.

"We're heading to Mamaw's house pretty soon."

"Does she live next door?" Hunter asked.

"No, that's my parents."

"You guys should just create a whole new town. Robertsonville. Or Duckville."

"Don't tell that to Willie," Korie joked. "He might think that's a good idea."

Two ugly sweaters still lay on John Luke's bed. Korie took the one with a stuffed Santa's head sticking out of its chest. "Now I like this. You'd be a big hit at the brunch if you wore this."

"I'd feel like an idiot."

Korie laughed. "You haven't seen Willie."

Either Hunter didn't get the joke or didn't necessarily care.

"Do I have to?" he asked.

"Of course not. It's just like duck hunting—I want you to feel like a part of our family."

"But I'm not."

"I know," Korie said. "But that doesn't mean you can't have fun like we do."

"You know how much fun I have with my family at Christmastime?"

She shook her head.

"None. Zero. Nada. It's kinda depressing, too. I sometimes used to think, 'Hey, people are out there having great old times.' Eventually I forgot about thinking like that. But being here brings back all those memories."

"I'm sorry, Hunter."

"I'm not saying that to make you feel bad."

Well, it's still making me feel bad.

"I'm just being honest," Hunter said.

So put on the sweater and stop sulking like a little toddler.

Korie would never say this to the kid. But she really wanted to. She wanted to say it and then add the whole "just being honest" thing.

But the slight annoyance was only temporary. She knew Hunter was struggling. That was exactly the reason he was there.

"Nobody is going to think you look foolish wearing those. I think they're pretty great myself."

"And you guys always do this?" Hunter asked. "Really?"

"Yeah. We really do. We're really slightly nutty."

"It's kinda cool to see," he said.

Before they left the room, Hunter picked up the Santa head sweater and slipped it on. As he adjusted it, his hair stuck out in different directions. "So how do I look?"

"Absolutely perfect," Korie said. "Great job."

Hunter grabbed the squishy Santa in his hand. "What if I get food on this?"

"I think we'll survive," she said.

He laughed, and once again Korie found herself thankful to hear that sound.

18
THE HOLLY and THE IVY and THE REDNECKS

"Wait a minute—that's your mother's mother?"

Several hours into the day and Hunter's head hurt.

"Technically it's called a 'grandmother,'" Willie said, passing by the conversation.

"Yes—this is my mother's mother," Korie said. "My grandmother."

This family was hard to keep track of. All the men had thick beards and wore camouflage. All the women looked like suburban mothers.

"I thought she was your mom," Hunter said.

Korie's grandmother gave him a smile and said how sweet of a compliment that was. She didn't know he was being completely serious.

"Does that mean *she's* your mom?" he asked Korie, pointing to another blonde-haired woman.

"Yep, that's right."

Hunter nodded, but he was totally lost. There was no way he'd remember all this, even though he'd already met some of these people the first day he got here.

The smells of different kinds of cookies waged war in the air. Hunter couldn't believe he was craving one even though his stomach was full of the amazing brunch they'd just eaten. They'd had egg quiche and grits and pancakes and ham and Orange Julius, and Hunter had enjoyed all of it. Yes, even the grits. Those creamy white things with the butter in them that looked odd but tasted pretty yummy.

What's happening to me? I'm using the word yummy.

Now he was baking cookies. Not just smelling them and getting ready to eat them but baking them.

He'd even volunteered to help.

Of course, everybody pitched in to make the cookies, but for some reason the black cloud Hunter had woken up with had vanished.

The moods came and went like that. A meteorologist would have a hard time keeping track of the storms coming and going in his soul. Some days would start with the forecast looking warm and sunny, and then somehow by midday there would be thunderstorms and hail and threats of tornadoes.

This day had started a bit like that. And Hunter hadn't even known why.

"He's a bit moody."

This was a phrase he'd grown accustomed to his parents saying. Not only about him but in front of him. It had become a tattoo he was used to wearing, one he couldn't get rid of even if he tried. "Moody Hunter" was just part of the territory. But still, this morning he'd woken up feeling annoyed. Feeling heavy. Feeling let down even though nobody had let anybody down.

He had thought that maybe the happy people were raining on his sad parade. So he'd dealt with it the way he usually did. By turning up the volume.

Unfortunately another reality had hit him.

Sometimes the songs weren't loud enough to drown out the silence in his spirit. It wasn't a Zen-like or Yoda-like silence but more of an empty, silent, scary kind. One he was painfully used to.

The Robertsons and their extended families didn't believe in silence. They didn't believe in cynicism. They weren't making fun of the neighbors. Well, maybe that's 'cause they were all each other's neighbors. But regardless, they weren't talking about Sammy across the street, who had problems. They weren't laughing at someone else's expense. They weren't feeling superior to anybody. They were simply having fun being with each other.

The storm clouds of this morning had somehow disappeared. Not literally—no. West Monroe was still supposed to get some sleet or snow tonight and maybe tomorrow on Christmas Day. But for Hunter, the sky was a soft sort of blue. Smiley, sorta cotton ball–white clouds were up there floating around. In his head and his heart.

Now I'm thinking about smiley cotton-ball clouds.

Maybe he was drinking the water, too. The West Monroe happy liquid.

He would like some of that. He could *use* some of that.

"Okay, we have some more cookies needing decorating," Korie's aunt Joneal called out.

Hunter volunteered and soon was making little pieces of art with dough and candy and frosting. There was an entire counter and tables full of decorative items for cookies. The creativity in this kitchen was cool. And Hunter was getting pretty proud of his creations, too.

Korie came over and looked at the cookies he'd made. "You're good at this."

"Thanks," he said.

"First cooking, now baking. See all the things you're learning?"

"Mom will be worried if I try this out in our kitchen," Hunter said.

"I think you should surprise her," Korie said. "I think she'd love to see you busy in the kitchen."

"Women like it when men cook for them," Willie said.

"That is very true," Korie said. "Take it from me."

"Surprise her." Hunter wondered if their idea could really work—and if he could really pull it off once he got home.

19
STEP into CHRISTMAS TROUBLE

Willie had disappeared. Again.

It was time to leave for church, yet somehow, for some reason, Willie had vanished.

Korie knew something was up. She just didn't know what it could be.

She'd first searched her aunt's house but hadn't found him. Then, after asking around, she'd texted him to see where he went. No response. She texted a couple more times. Now she was calling him. Not out of concern—it wasn't like she feared he'd lost his mind and run off. It just wasn't like him not to tell her when he'd be gone. Maybe Willie truly was planning a surprise.

The phone rang three times before he picked up. "Yeah?"

"Hey. Where are you?"

"Aw," Willie said. "Do you miss me that much?"

"Where'd you go?"

"I'm around."

He was *so* up to something.

"Willie . . ."

"Can't you let a guy check out luxury cars in order to surprise his wife on Christmas morning?"

"Well, I happen to know this particular *guy*, and I know he'd never do such a thing."

Willie laughed. "Did the party stop after I left?"

"No. Not even close."

"That hurts."

She laughed. "So when are you going to be home?"

He didn't respond, which made him seem busy.

"Oh, I'm sorry," Korie joked. "Did I catch you at a bad time?"

"Yeah, in fact, you kind of did."

"This better be good," Korie said.

"What better be good?"

"Whatever it is that you're keeping from me."

"Just trust me," he told her.

"I always do."

"Then why are you calling now?"

"To remind you about church."

"I'll be there."

As always when he was planning something, Willie sounded confident and full of himself. Which made her curious why he was so confident and full of himself this time. But she reminded herself that his surprises were often really great.

Korie told herself not to worry. For the moment.

She would start worrying if something began to burn and smoke could be seen. Or if the police and ambulances pulled into their driveway.

20
ROBERTSONS WE HAVE HEARD ON HIGH

Hunter couldn't remember the last time he'd been at a church. Maybe for his cousin's wedding. Or an uncle's funeral. But that was about it. Now he sat in the pew of White's Ferry Road Church with five hundred relatives of the Robertsons surrounding him. At least that's how many it seemed like at first. The other Robertson brothers and their families were around and they had similar-looking families too. Eventually Hunter noticed the rest of the congregation, and he was relieved to see people of diverse backgrounds wearing everything from business suits to camo shirts. Several people welcomed him, but still—everybody knew everybody, and Hunter couldn't help feeling out of place.

There was a lot of singing and some reading from the Bible, and the preacher got up and shared some thoughts. But Hunter couldn't focus. This had always been a problem, ever since he was young. It sometimes happened when he was in class, but it was also an issue when his mother or father was talking to him. The person who was speaking would sound something like this in Hunter's head: *"Hunter, you know you need to really get started hamamamamamamama . . ."*

He couldn't help but tune the rest of the world out at times.

The events of Christmas still felt like a flock of birds flying overhead. They seemed real and obviously were headed in some certain direction, but soon they were gone and never thought of again. And this holiday was a lot like that. Maybe there really was a baby named Jesus born in a manger years ago, but Hunter wasn't there to see and touch him. He couldn't hear the baby's cries. And he definitely didn't know whether God was this baby's father. How *could* he know? Really and truly?

Yet all these people around him—did they really and truly believe it? Or were they just sitting there watching the birds pass overhead as well?

Another musical number, another reading.

Hunter wasn't totally sure what all was happening after church. They were going to hang out with Korie's family for a while, but maybe then it would be time to open gifts. Hunter didn't know if the Robertsons got him anything, but he was sure it would be awkward either way—opening gifts from a family he barely knew or sitting there as everyone opened presents around him. But at least there was no magic with presents. No supernatural faith was needed to believe in them.

Can't we just get out of here? Presents I believe in. Feeling the wrapping paper and tearing it away and opening the box and seeing what's inside.

A girl maybe a few years older than Hunter went up on stage and began singing. He was getting impatient with the service, but for the moment he stopped thinking about the pew or the church or the presents.

Hunter had never heard this song before, but it instantly pricked at him for some reason. He'd expected the Christmas carols and church hymns, but not this.

It was a sad song. A lonely song. A perfect song for him.

The narrator of the song was traveling and tired. She was cold and sounded pretty desperate.

It took Hunter a few moments to realize this was supposed to be Mary telling her story.

Mary, the mother of Jesus.

And for the first time ever, Hunter realized that if there really had been a Mary, then she must have been frightened. Possibly freaked out. He'd never thought of her in this way. But a new experience and a new place and a new everything brought out fears in anybody. That's what Mary was going through in this song.

She was frightened by the load she had to bear.

Yeah, I can relate.

A world as cold as stone. Walking a path completely alone.

Yep.

Seemingly out of fortune and out of luck and out of breath . . .

Breath of heaven.

Something weird happened.

Hunter got goose bumps on his skin. And tears in his eyes.

Something was wrong. They must have spiked his lemonade this afternoon or put something in the cookie mix. How could he get this emotional? This sappy and silly?

Yet he kept listening. He tried to casually wipe his eyes and hope nobody noticed.

He took a breath and wished faith could be as easy as it sounded in this song. He wished it could be that simple.

A simple breath. Of hope. Of light. Of goodness.

Yeah, as imaginary as Santa Claus and his reindeer.

But something told Hunter maybe he was wrong. Maybe these people surrounding him were right.

Maybe they'd experienced that breath of heaven, and that's why they were here and why they were doing all of this. The gifts and the baking and the gathering and the greetings.

Yeah. Maybe.

But the song ended and Hunter knew so would his time in West Monroe.

It was a nice dream. Like thinking and hoping you'd get some perfect present on Christmas morning only to finally open it and see something far less valuable, far less cool, far less everything than you expected.

Some people lived in the center of the dream. But most lived in the farther-away sections. Always trying to get to the middle. Always trying but never quite making it.

21

CHESTNUTS and CHICAGOANS ROASTING on an OPEN FIRE

"You're in for a treat tonight."

Korie turned to look at Hunter, who was riding in the back with Rebecca, Will, and Bella as they returned home. Church had ended about twenty minutes ago, and it had taken almost all that time just to greet different people and wish everyone she saw a merry Christmas. She had even seen her aunt Mary in the restroom and had held a nice brief conversation with her. There was never enough time to catch up around Christmas, especially since they still had a big evening ahead of them.

"I bet there's food connected to it somehow," Hunter said in his deadpan tone.

"Always!" Willie yelled as he drove.

"We're going to have dinner at my parents' house next door. And then the rest of the fun begins."

"Should I be scared?" Hunter asked.

"Terrified," Willie answered. "You better get a plane back to Chicago right now. Or you'll be changed. Forever."

"Stop. He's just kidding around. It's fun. We play games and then we—"

"Don't spoil it," Willie said.

"I'm just telling him what we're going to be doing."

"Nobody likes a spoiler. Right, gang?"

The three Robertson kids who were present agreed with Willie in unison.

"It'll be fun," Korie told Hunter. "I promise."

Willie made a *mwahaha* sound but never turned his head toward Hunter. Korie could only imagine what the boy was thinking.

After a buffet dinner of sandwiches and chips and veggies and dips and other assorted things that you could assemble on your paper plate, the games began. The family all shuffled from the large kitchen—where some had been sitting and others standing—into the main room, where the over-size dining room table was located, along with the Christmas tree and the sofas and chairs. As always, Korie's mother, Chrys—whom everyone called Two-Mama—introduced the games.

"Before our talent show, we're going to play a round of charades. This time we're doing obscure Christmas movies. Most of these are probably movies you've never heard of before. You'll have to act them out without saying a single word. And since we have a guest here—everybody has met Hunter, right?—we all have to be on our *best* behavior."

There were laughs and moans and boos.

"Now for the teams," Chrys said.

Hunter ended up on a team with Willie, which meant he couldn't just be a wallflower who was forgotten about. This was a relief to Korie, who found herself assigned to a team with Sadie, her aunt, and a cousin.

Soon the insanity began.

Korie's uncle Jeremy fell to the ground, pretending to be dead. His team guessed the movie right away: *Better Off Dead*.

Willie went to the front and held up two fingers. Then he proceeded to act like a crazy person, making everybody guess wild things.

"One Flew Over the Cuckoo's Nest!"

Hunter didn't say anything at first. The others on his team kept guessing while Willie acted creepy and weird.

Soon they realized the second word was *Santa*. Then it became a free-for-all of Santa descriptors.

"Bad Santa!"

"Mad Santa!"

"Uncle Si Santa!"

Willie pretended to hold a knife and made a stabbing gesture.

"*Psycho Santa*," Hunter finally said.

Willie jumped over and gave Hunter a high-five hug. It was really an attempt at a high-five that spontaneously morphed into a bear hug. Korie could see Hunter turning white, either from the embarrassment or from the lack of oxygen going to his head.

The one movie that stumped John Luke's team was a two-word title that had the word *nuts* in it. John Luke acted crazy, like his father had, and pretended to be eating and cracking nuts. Everybody got that. But they were stumped on the first word.

John Luke pointed to Sadie and to his grandfather. Then he waved away that clue.

Next he acted like he was stirring something; then he acted confused. That really threw his team off.

"*Totally Nuts!*"

"*Going Nuts!*"

Things began to take a turn for the worse until time ran out.

"It was *Mixed Nuts*," John Luke said.

"Where did you get these movies?" Korie asked her mother.

"The beauty of googling strange Christmas movies. There were some pretty disturbing ones I didn't even list."

Finally it was Hunter's turn to go up in front of everybody. He first said no, but Willie practically carried him up to the Christmas tree to play out the charade. It was obvious not only that Hunter was uncomfortable, but also that he'd never played this particular game before.

"Okay, so it's six words," he started to say.

"You can't talk," Sadie said, laughing.

"Oh, okay. Well, it's—"

He remembered again and nodded. He raised six fingers. Then held his hands in front of his stomach as if he had a belly.

"Mary," Willie said.

"Willie?" a cousin guessed.

This got everybody laughing.

Soon they guessed it was Santa.

Hunter jumped around and acted like a rabbit.

"Bunny."

He nodded and pretended to lick something held in his hand.

"Ice cream!"

But Hunter must not have considered that he needed to act out the words in order. He tried to communicate the sequence, but time was going fast.

"Santa Claus kills a bunny with ice cream!" Willie shouted.

Hunter shook his head, pointed, and turned red, and Korie could tell he was frustrated.

Then time ran out.

"What movie was that?" Willie said in disbelief.

Hunter sighed. "I messed up."

"Aw, man, come on. It's fine."

Hunter went to sit back down.

"What was it?" Willie asked again.

"*Santa and the Ice Cream Bunny*."

Willie stopped him. "Hold on. That doesn't even make sense. We need a redo."

"That's all the movies," Chrys said.

"No. He had *Santa and the Ice Cream Bunny*."

"It was my fault," she said.

"We win just because that's the dumbest name for a movie. Ever."

Korie watched Hunter and could tell he felt a little better about his attempt at the game. Willie continued to plead his case and make everybody laugh.

"Santa doesn't want an ice cream bunny," Willie said. "There's absolutely no reason why he'd want an ice cream bunny."

"Okay, okay," Korie said, trying to turn the volume down a bit. "Is it time for the talent show?"

She looked over and saw Hunter sinking into the sofa he was sitting on.

"Don't worry," she said to him over half a dozen speaking voices.

He nodded and glanced around the room. She

wouldn't have been surprised if he stood and bolted out the front door.

We can't be that scary. This can't be that abnormal.

But thinking of his situation at home and how he was abruptly thrown into this group like a plum tossed into . . .

A bowl of mixed nuts.

She smiled at the silly thought. She would have to share it with Willie later. He would laugh.

But for now she wanted to figure out how to make Hunter laugh.

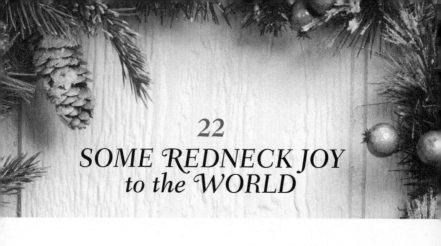

22
SOME REDNECK JOY
to the WORLD

Once half the room of about fortysome people began chanting Hunter's name, he knew there was no way out of it. So he stood and walked to the front of the crowd.

"I don't really have any talents," he said.

Which was very true. He couldn't sing or dance or put on any kind of drama. He was horrible at telling jokes and even worse at telling stories.

There is one thing I can do. . . .

"You can do *anything* you want," Willie said from the back.

"This is a safe crowd," Korie's mother encouraged with a sweet smile.

The room was packed, and Hunter now stood close to the Christmas tree. Already there had been great acts from everybody. John Luke and Sadie sang a song from the Christmas album the Robertsons had put out. Will beatboxed. Bella sang a popular song with one of her cousins. And Rebecca played the piano.

There had been readings and a card trick and even one of the cousins standing on her head.

And I'm following all of that by standing up in front of these people trying to think of something.

"Anything you want to do," Korie's father, John, repeated from the back of the room.

Hunter nodded, then scanned the room for something ideal to use. "I need a prop."

John Luke pushed Sadie to the front. "Here. Use her."

Hunter shook his head. "No, not—I need something. Not someone."

He noticed a barstool that someone was sitting

on. It was average height and weight, at least from what Hunter could see.

"Can I borrow that for a second?"

Once he picked up the barstool, a thought went through his mind. *This is a bad idea, man.*

But the whole family was watching and smiling and waiting to see what he was going to do.

"I'm going to balance this on my head," he told them as he continued to examine the wooden stool in his hand. The seat was cushiony, and that worried him a bit.

The crowd began to clap and call his name.

No going back now, you idiot.

He lifted the stool and gently set it on his head. "Just a minute—I usually warm up before doing this."

"You got this, Hunter!" Willie shouted.

Hunter looked around him and asked for a little more space. Then he adjusted the stool on his head and held it with both hands for a moment.

"Just one more sec," he said. Moving his head. Positioning his legs and the rest of his body. Then carefully and slowly starting to move less and less.

With the four-foot-tall barstool on his head, he let go and balanced it totally hands-free.

And for seven glorious seconds, he was doing it. Until it began to fall to the side. *Right* into the Christmas tree.

And he wasn't fast enough to stop it.

The barstool crashed down into ornaments and garlands and pine sap. It took down three rows of lights before coming to a thudding stop. The sound of breaking glass was heard. The tree's lights flickered once, then went out.

A chorus of gasps and "Oops!" "Oh no!" and "Yikes!" filled the family room.

Then Hunter let out a nice doozy of a curse. He couldn't help it. And everyone was staring at him.

"Man, it's okay," Willie started to say.

"Don't worry about the tree," Two-Mama said, coming to his side.

Others were approaching him too, and they gave him smiles and "Don't worry about it" comments and backslaps, but it was done and Hunter was done. He felt like a complete moron.

Told you so, didn't I?

He helped pick up the barstool and the tree decorations that littered the floor. What he really wanted to do was bash the stool against the wall and toss the bits into the nearby fire.

"Okay, okay, it's all fun and games until someone hurls something into the tree," Willie said, striding to the front of the room. "Our guest is certainly mortified—as he should be, since those are our great-great-grandmother's ornaments he just busted up."

Willie let out a laugh and slapped Hunter on his back. "Man, I'm kidding. I do worse every year. No joke. You had that thing balanced for a second. Which was fun to see. Let's everybody give Hunter a big round of applause."

Hunter made his way to the back of the room before Willie could call him up again.

"Now, don't you go disappearing or anything, Hunter. You gotta stay and watch this."

Hunter slipped into the very farthest corner of the room, as if he were trying to find a way behind the walls. Willie grabbed a pretend microphone and put on a gigantic hat.

"Well, talk about perfect timing," Willie said. "Christmas is all about joy, right? 'Joy to the World' and all that? So in celebration of Christmas and kids from Chicago destroying Christmas trees— aw, man, Hunter, you know I'm kidding, right? In honor of this joyful season, I'm going to sing a little song."

Hunter thought he'd seen that big hat on Willie's head sometime before but he didn't remember when or why. Then the song started, and Willie began singing karaoke.

The song was "Happy" by Pharrell Williams.

"'Because I'm happy,'" he sang.

Willie didn't sound good, exactly. But it didn't seem to matter what he sounded like. Which was sort of awesome in a funny way.

All the kids came up beside Willie and began clapping, and soon everybody was singing and dancing together.

For the moment, Hunter just laughed and forgot

about his mishap with the stool and the tree and the juggling that wasn't meant to be. He actually found himself clapping too because, yeah, it was what he wanted to do.

Willie kept singing and even the adults were clapping now, and Hunter was pretty sure he might not ever have another Christmas Eve like this in his whole life.

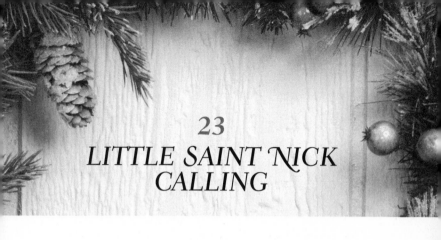

23
LITTLE SAINT NICK CALLING

"Hey, Mom."

There was a pause for some reason.

"Hunter—how are you?" Mom sounded surprised. And tired.

"I'm okay."

"Are you having a lot of fun?"

"Yeah, sure," he said.

Another pause. Hunter wondered what Mom was up to.

"I miss you a lot," she said.

She sounded sad.

Is she crying?

"Are you okay?"

"Yeah. Just having some parental doubts. Nothing unusual. My hourly dark night of the soul."

Hunter never knew what to say when his mother talked like this. He was the kid. He was the one who needed advice from her. He had no idea how to give her motivation or encouragement or support.

Maybe you could just tell her you love her, you moron.

"So what'd you do today?" Mom asked, trying to suddenly sound upbeat.

He told her about the brunch and making cookies and going to church. He spoke so fast that Mom had to interrupt him.

"This was all just today?"

"Yeah," Hunter said.

"What'd you think of church?"

"They baptized me," he said.

"Are you serious?"

"No." He laughed. He loved fooling his mother,

and the older he got, the more he could pull her leg. "We played charades tonight and then had a talent competition."

"Hang on—you had a what?"

"A talent competition," Hunter said.

"What did you do?"

"Well, I tried to balance a barstool on my head."

"That's great!"

Hunter laughed. "Yeah. It was for a second. Then it fell. Into the Christmas tree."

"What?"

"Yeah," he said.

"Wait a minute," Mom said. "Hunter—did you really do that?"

"Are you saying I don't have talent?"

She laughed. "No, but I know how you are in groups."

"This isn't an ordinary group."

"I should say not. I'm glad to hear it."

"Uh-huh," he said. "Then Willie Robertson ended up doing a whole routine around Pharrell Williams's song 'Happy.'"

"Who?" Mom knew nothing about music or movies or any pop culture.

"It's okay. It was pretty crazy."

"So you are having fun?" she asked.

"Yeah. I guess. I don't know."

"Have you spoken with your father?"

"No."

"I heard from them today. Sounds like they're having a great time."

The words were simple, but they still stung.

"Having a great time."

"Yeah, well, I need to go," Hunter said.

He didn't want to talk anymore. He especially didn't want to hear about his father and his brother.

"I'm glad you're doing okay, Hunter."

I'm okay but I'm definitely not great.

"Yeah. Thanks."

This would be the moment. The moment to tell her he missed her.

But I don't. Not really.

The moment to give her something. To reach

out and say something, anything, just one simple thing.

"Okay, then. Talk to you later." That was all Hunter said.

It wasn't all he felt and meant and wanted to say, but it was the only thing that would come out of his mouth.

"Merry Christmas, Hunter. I'll call you tomorrow, okay?"

"Okay."

He said good-bye and stared at the dark, blank screen on his phone.

It felt like looking in the mirror.

He heard laughter in the background but didn't want to go back in there. He didn't feel like laughing or playing or celebrating or doing anything like that.

Hunter simply wanted to get out of there.

So he did. He grabbed his jacket from the other room and slipped out the side door without being noticed.

24
O COME,
ALL YE SKEPTICAL

Midnight approached and the house was finally
quiet. The Robertsons had put out Christmas
cookies and milk like always. Korie had spent the
last half hour arranging the presents from Santa.
Each kid received one unwrapped present along
with wrapped gifts in their stockings and under
the tree.

While finishing up with the gifts, she heard
footsteps rustling down the stairs. For a minute she
thought it might be John Luke, but instead Hunter
appeared.

"Everything all right?" she asked him.

"Yeah," he said, rubbing his hands together in a nervous fashion.

"Do you need anything?"

He shook his head. "No. I'm good." Hunter looked at the cookies and milk as if he was unsure why they were there. He had been upstairs when the kids put them out.

"That's our tradition every year. For Santa." She raised her eyebrows at him and smiled.

"Oh, cool."

Hunter looked as if he had something he wanted to tell her. Korie knew. After raising five children along with lots of nieces and nephews, she recognized that kind of look.

"You doing okay?"

"I was wondering . . ."

"Wondering about what?"

"Was I picked randomly? To come down here?"

Korie had wondered if Hunter might eventually ask this. She had even thought about what she might or might not say.

But now she didn't hesitate to answer.

"I received an e-mail from your mother. I read it and it made me cry."

Hunter gave her a funny look. "I thought she just entered the contest and I was chosen."

Korie shook her head. "No."

"What did the e-mail say?"

"You might need to ask your mother. I don't think I should share it, especially if she doesn't want me to."

"It was probably something like, 'Dear Robertsons: My son is messed up and he's a loser who hasn't ever experienced a true Christmas because we're a family of losers.'"

"No. Not at all."

"How bad was it?" Hunter asked.

Korie smiled. "It wasn't about whether it was bad or good. I felt she was being authentic. She thought highly of our family, but she wasn't focused on the fame. Which I kinda liked. Some people only want to capitalize on our spotlight. But your mother—the spotlight she wanted was solely on you."

Hunter looked surprised. "My mother? Seriously?"

"Yeah. It sounded . . . She said things have been tough for you guys. For you especially."

He looked down but didn't say anything.

"I know holidays are hard times for lots of people. And after reading her letter, I thought you'd really enjoy coming down here."

"I have. Even if—if I don't act like it."

"Thank you for saying that, Hunter. Now you better get some rest," Korie said. "Another big day tomorrow."

Hunter started to head upstairs, then stopped for a second and turned around. "Thanks for telling me."

"Sure. Good night, Hunter."

25
HAPPY CHRISTMAS (PARTY IS OVER)

"I wouldn't worry about what happened tonight," John Luke said when Hunter walked back into the room.

"I destroyed your grandparents' Christmas tree," he replied as he sat on the cot. "Yeah, sure, no problem. Good thing two hundred of your relatives weren't there. Oh, wait."

"At least it wasn't tomorrow night."

"Why's that?" Hunter asked.

"We're going to Papaw Phil and Miss Kay's house. If you think my dad was giving you a hard time, you should hear my uncles."

"No thanks. Think I'll pass on that."

John Luke laughed. "Dad was just teasing. He likes to joke around. Mom says he only picks on those he loves—if he didn't like you, he would probably just leave you alone."

Hunter stared at the picture of the Rocky Mountains on the wall behind John Luke's bed. "My dad likes to be gone."

John Luke went over to a shelf in the corner and grabbed a couple of shoe boxes. "Hey, I have something I want to read to you."

He put the boxes on the bed and opened the first one. Inside were a handful of letters. John Luke glanced at them, then replaced the lid. "It's not this box. It's the other one."

The next box he opened contained flyers and notes of some kind. A big stack of them.

"What's all that?"

"These are sermon notes from the last two years."

Hunter just stared at the giant wad of paper John Luke was sorting through.

"Sermon notes? As in going-to-church-on-Sunday notes?"

"Yeah. Some from Wednesday nights or camps I've gone to."

"Wow," Hunter said. "You've been to a lot of sermons."

Hunter could see handwriting on each of the pamphlets in the box too. Writing that was obviously John Luke's.

Once again, Hunter was in disbelief. Who was this guy? "John Luke—are you for real? Like seriously?"

"What do you mean?" he asked, focused on the papers he was going through.

"I mean—come on. There must be something you're hiding. Are you a part of a strange cult in the backwoods? Or maybe you're the father of three children nobody knows about. Or you have a meth lab somewhere you're not telling anybody about."

John Luke gave him a nod and a total serious face. "Yeah. I *do* have a meth lab. But don't tell my parents. They wouldn't like it."

This actually got a genuine laugh from Hunter. It was exactly something he might say.

"It's just—I have friends back home, and I go to their room and they're showing me weird stuff on their computer. You know. But you have a shoe box of sermon notes."

"Here it is," John Luke said, withdrawing the handout he'd been looking for. "This was from a year ago or so. We had a doctor come speak at our church who had gone to places like Haiti to help those in need after the earthquake. He was talking about the difference that joy can make in a person—how it can really be healing having joy in your heart. He read this Bible verse, Proverbs 17:22: 'A cheerful heart is good medicine, but a broken spirit saps a person's strength.'"

"Are you saying I'm not cheery enough?" Hunter asked, partly joking and partly not.

"No, not at all. I'm just saying—that made me think of my dad. And our family. And I believe it's true. A cheerful heart is a lot like medicine."

"I can't take all your cheerful hearts back with me to Chicago, you know. No room on the plane."

"Yeah, I know, but in a way you can."

"Maybe I'd be cheery too if I lived here." Hunter paused, then added, "Maybe I'd take lots of sermon notes."

"I write them down so I don't forget."

"I write down lyrics from songs I like."

"That's cool," John Luke said. "I'm going to go brush my teeth."

Hunter sat gazing at the Colorado mountains for a long time. Thinking about this thing called joy. Thinking about being happy.

It was hard. Being cheerful when the backbone of your life felt a little like Jell-O. Being happy when there was nobody to be happy around. Being content when every moment of your life you were wishing and wanting and wondering when good things were going to come your way.

Sometimes he felt like he was in the poster on the wall. The serene mountains were in the background of his life, and he could see them in all their beauty. But Hunter was still standing on flat land, looking from afar. Knowing there was no way he could ever get on top of those glorious peaks.

26

I HEARD the SCREAMS
on CHRISTMAS DAY

Korie awoke just as the sun began to peek through
the blinds in their bedroom. She looked around but
noticed Willie had already woken up and slipped
out of the room.

What's he up to?

She put on her robe and slippers and headed
toward the kitchen. She smelled something odd.
Something that was truly foul. Like a combination
of a forest fire and an outhouse.

When she reached the smoky kitchen, she

saw some monstrous carcass of an animal on
the island.

"Hey, Korie. I'm just cooking everyone a surprise
Christmas breakfast." Willie was wearing only his
boxers and an apron. Oh, he also had on some
boots and his bandanna.

"What are you doing?"

"I'm cooking a special treat I've been saving for
today."

"It smells awful. And looks even worse."

"This," Willie said, pointing at the skinned
animal, "is a yak."

"A what?"

"A yak."

"A yak?" Korie asked.

"Yes, a yak."

"This isn't a yak."

"Yes, it's a yak."

It was almost like the conversation was on a
loop. Like a song. *Yakety-yak-yak.*

"Where are the kids?"

"Oh, we have a problem, Houston," Willie said.

"What do you mean?"

"I mean—well, it's better if you just look."

"Look where?" she asked.

"In the family room."

She went in there and found Hunter passed out on the couch. Crumbs from the Christmas cookies were on his clothes. His mouth had dried milk around it.

Oh yeah, and every single Christmas present had been opened. Every last one.

"Hunter!"

She couldn't believe what had happened. Their Christmas was ruined. And this terror of a teen had done it.

He opened his eyes and slowly sat up. Then he started to laugh at her. Korie began to turn but saw Willie in the kitchen, holding a meat cleaver and laughing as well.

And the rest of the kids were standing by the window, waving at her, laughing.

It was snowing outside. But the snow was made of little pink crystals . . .

Korie sat up in one of those gasping, choking, head-spinning awakenings—the darkness all around saying it was only a dream. She breathed in and out and heard Willie's light snoring.

Good. No Willie cooking up a yak. No Hunter hungover on Christmas cookies and opening presents. No pink snow.

She let her heart stop racing and knew it was just the busyness of the holiday making her this way. That and worries for their guest.

As she put her head against the pillow, she prayed, asking God to give them a good day tomorrow. Not a day full of getting what they wanted, but a day where they could see God's face shining on them. It always did on Christmas, and that was the whole point.

She prayed that somehow, someway, it would shine on Hunter too. And maybe he'd stop and be filled with a little sense of wonder and awe.

Maybe. Hopefully.

She prayed he would. That all of them would.

27
DUCKIN' AROUND
the CHRISTMAS TREE

The pine tree looked perfect in its triangular shape, and it glowed as Hunter approached. Everybody was already in there waiting for him. His hair was still wet from the shower and his head was fuzzy from the deep sleep he'd gotten. He didn't know what to expect today, but he wasn't thinking ahead, either. He was going to try to take John Luke's advice about having a cheerful heart. Maybe it really would be good medicine for his soul.

He wondered if there would be a framed picture of the Robertsons that they'd sign and give to him

along with personalized key chains featuring their
faces and . . .

A cheerful heart. Not a cynical one.

"Merry Christmas!" everyone said in a collective
voice as he entered.

Sometimes he wanted to go against the grain
and not be like everybody and not have to say those
two words everyone said over and over again at this
time of year. But today he decided to grin and bear
it. "Merry Christmas," he replied.

To Hunter's surprise, the Robertsons did not
appear as photograph-ready as he'd expected. All of
them were still in their pajamas. John Luke had a
terrible case of bedhead. There was no makeup or
styled hair in sight. Hunter fit right in.

Looking around at all of these people who
were no longer strangers to him, Hunter found
himself glad to be here. Glad for the connections
he'd made. Glad not to feel so alone on another
Christmas morning.

But you're not gonna be here for long. . . .

He shrugged off that nagging voice in him

that never seemed to go away. That emotional bully bringing him down. Today he was going to be free.

Or at least he was going to try as hard as he could to feel that way.

"Santa" brought Hunter a Kindle e-reader that was unexpected and really over-the-top.

"I guess Santa thinks you might want to read some books," Korie said with a smile. "I bet he put some of his favorites on there, too."

And yes, she was right. There were about a dozen titles listed on the device. Some he'd heard of before, like *To Kill a Mockingbird*, and others he hadn't, such as *Love Does* and *The Purpose Driven Life*. Maybe Korie had seen him reading the worn-out paperback horror novel he'd brought and figured he liked to read.

"Thanks," he said, not sure whom to thank specifically. "This is really . . ."

He hadn't bought presents for any of them. He'd

never have guessed they would treat him like one of their own.

"I didn't end up—"

"Oh, it's okay," Korie said. "Don't think anything of it."

It was fun taking turns with Will and Bella and Rebecca and Sadie and John Luke, opening presents from under the tree and in their stockings. He even discovered his own stocking with *Hunter* stitched across it.

Too much.

He received some things that he might have expected, of course. A Duck Commander cap. A Duck Commander sweatshirt. A Duck Commander jacket.

"You can never have enough Duck Commander stuff," Willie said after Hunter held up a pair of Duck Commander boxers.

Hunter laughed, remembering how he'd asked Willie if they sold those.

"You are gonna be representing when you get back home," Willie said.

"I hope there's a Duck Commander rifle in one of these packages," Hunter joked.

"We might've, but that would never get through security."

He got an iTunes gift card from John Luke, a funky-looking scarf from Rebecca, an LSU T-shirt from Will, and a set of cooking spices from Bella. Willie handed him one more present that was from Sadie.

"We almost missed this one," he said.

Hunter unwrapped it just like the others. As he opened it, he saw Sadie's big and beautiful smile beaming back at him.

It was a framed photo of her.

Autographed.

Hunter could literally feel the tidal wave of red washing over his face as he attempted a smile and forced himself to look at Sadie.

"Thanks," he said in a mouse-like voice.

"What is that?" Sadie said, jumping up and grabbing the picture. "Who did this?"

For a second, Hunter felt like he would pass out.

He could hear the laughing and Sadie's screaming and the sudden chaos the picture inspired.

"Dad! You did this!"

Willie just sat there with a big grin peeking out under his thick beard. "I don't know what you're talking about."

"That was mean," Korie said. "Hunter, I'm sorry."

"It's fine," he said.

"I am so embarrassed," Sadie said. "I did not do this. I'm mortified."

"It's a good picture," Hunter said.

Then he felt stupid for saying so. *Just keep your mouth shut. Please.*

He actually did get a gift from Sadie, and it was a picture, but not of her. Someone had taken a photo of Hunter, Phil, Willie, John Luke, Uncle Si, and Jase after their day of hunting. The image was framed.

"Thanks," Hunter said, less awkwardly this time.

"A memory of your first true hunt," Willie said.

And then it was time for him to unwrap the final gift. He couldn't shake the feeling of a spotlight shining in his face over and over again. People he didn't really know looking at him and watching him open presents *they'd* given him.

"I'm sorry I didn't give you guys anything," Hunter said, holding the rectangular package in his hands.

"You gave us yourself," Korie said.

Hunter let out a laugh. "Yeah. Sorry about that."

"Go ahead—keep opening it," she replied.

He tore off the golden wrapping paper, revealing a leather book. Then, looking at the spine, he realized it was a Bible.

"We would've given you a Duck Commander Bible, but I forgot," Willie said.

Hunter wasn't sure if he was joking or not, but he nodded. "Thanks."

He noticed a name engraved on the leather in the lower right-hand corner.

HUNTER JAMES CLARKE

"It's got my name on it," he said.

"We hope you like it," Korie said.

"We put the name on the cover so you can't sell it," Willie added.

"He's just kidding." Korie shook her head.

The leather book felt heavy in his hand. He didn't know exactly what he was going to do with it, but he still appreciated the thought.

Well, you know, you could read *it.*

He wanted to tell them all how much he appreciated this. These things. But more than just the items surrounding him, he wanted to thank *them* for surrounding him. For bringing some noise into his silent world. For bringing smiles when he rarely found any inside his home. For bringing laughter when his television and iPhone rarely supplied it. Maybe even for bringing love in a world that seemed to have lost it underneath the Christmas tree somewhere.

28

JOHN LUKE'S LAST CHRISTMAS

Christmas was a time steeped in tradition, and having Hunter here with her family reminded Korie of this. It seemed like every single tradition that came up, whether it was decorating cookies or setting some of them out for Santa Claus to eat, was a total surprise for Hunter. She wondered what kind of Christmas he normally had and imagined it was a fairly solitary one. But Korie knew that even big families could have empty holidays.

The joy didn't come in the presents you opened or the food you ate. It came in thanking those who gave them to you and in laughing with those you ate alongside of. And ultimately it came in knowing all of you were there for a purpose.

Not a ho-ho-ho but a hallelujah.

"Hark! the herald angels sing, 'Glory to the newborn King; peace on earth, and mercy mild, God and sinners reconciled!'"

She could hear the song playing in the background as the extended family assembled at her parents' house once again for one of her favorite traditions. They were having breakfast as they often did, but the reason she loved this particular breakfast was because everybody had a special plate they ate from. Plates she had actually helped make. And once again she'd included Hunter in this tradition by making him his own plate.

When she presented the plate with his name on it, she explained the tradition. "We each have our own. Some of them are what—ten, twenty years old? It's just another reminder of our family and what we have to be thankful for."

Hunter held his plate as if it were some precious

heirloom he might break. "Do we eat off them?" he asked.

"No, no, no," Willie said, standing nearby. "No, they're for decorative purposes only."

Of course Willie had his plate in hand, and it was full of eggs, biscuits, hash browns, and waffles.

"Absolutely no food on the plates!" he said as he made his way to the long dining room table.

"Like always, *don't* listen to him," Korie told Hunter.

The late breakfast on Christmas morning wasn't as large as the festivities last night. There were only about twenty people here. But there was so much to eat. Homemade blueberry muffins. Freshly baked biscuits. Scrambled eggs. Waffles. Homemade chocolate chip pancakes. Even fancy champagne glasses for orange juice.

Yes, the month after Christmas usually meant eating well and getting on the treadmill along with going to the doctor to check your heart. But for now, the scents and the sounds and the tastes were truly wonderful.

Before filling her plate, Korie glanced over and saw Hunter's plate. He had probably enough food on there to feed five people. She just smiled.

Good for you.

She was glad to see him finally starting to fit in.

The game room was full of torn wrapping paper and tissue paper and toys and tools and ten thousand other presents. The group of twenty people—including Korie's brother and sister and their families—had joked and talked and shouted and thanked each other for the last hour as they opened their Christmas presents. As always, it made Korie feel full. Just like breakfast. Stuffed with love. Overwhelmed with fellowship and feel-good emotions.

Soon they'd be heading back home to take a little break before going to Phil and Miss Kay's house this afternoon to celebrate Christmas with the Robertsons. They would all have a few hours to take naps, and Korie was looking forward to it after staying up late last night with all the preparations.

"Okay, everybody, I need a minute here," Willie said, standing in the center of the room.

Uh-oh.

"I have a big announcement."

Several people teased him and said this might be awful. Korie thought maybe he had some wacky Christmas present that he was going to bring out now. You never knew what to expect with Willie Robertson.

"I need everybody to go into the other room for a special video I made."

"What? We already have every season of the show," one of the cousins said.

"No, no, it's not that. Just—before we all leave, I have one more Christmas present to share."

I hope this won't be too embarrassing.

It took everybody a few minutes to go from the game room back to the large family room. This was the same room where the tree was located, the same place where Hunter had tried balancing a stool on his head. A large flat-screen television was attached to one wall, making this a place Willie,

Korie, and the kids often came to watch television or movies.

When everybody was situated, Willie went to the front of the room. He gave Korie a smile that made her nervous. She returned it but shook her head.

I'm going to kill him if he embarrasses me.

"Okay, so I'm going to ask John Luke to come up here and stand beside me."

John Luke looked surprised but got up and joined Willie.

"As some of you know, this is our last official Christmas with John Luke before he goes off to college," Willie began with his arm around his oldest son. "And as some of you also know, *some* people in our family have had a few moments of— well, let's just say they're not handling John Luke's leaving as well as the rest of us."

Everybody, including Willie and John Luke, looked at Korie.

"What are you talking about?" she said. "I'm handling it fine."

Willie nodded. "Uh, sure. Well, anyway, I've been working on something for a while. And I'm not any kind of moviemaker. I'm no Jep Robertson. But I did make a fun little video of John Luke to share with all of you. Especially those who are going to miss him a lot . . . Korie and Two-Mama."

This is why he's been going MIA all the time. Willie's been working on this video. A video that's really for me.

The movie began by playing some sweet, heartfelt music. Korie realized it was the theme song from *Finding Nemo*.

Suddenly Korie was spiraling back in time to October 11, 1995, when John Luke was born. On the video she could see herself holding the newborn. This tiny flower of a baby, her own smile so big after a long delivery. Next Willie showed up on the screen, holding John Luke in his arms.

The gift of life. So small and so precious.

Soon the snapshots in the video started to overwhelm Korie. It felt like she was seeing a thousand photos, along with ten thousand links to different memories. A hundred thousand emotions holding hands with a million different melodies. So many songs filled with so many different words. Happy and sad and funny and busy, but more than anything else, they made her thankful.

Life really does pass in a blink, doesn't it?

The newborn on the screen was now taller than her, and soon he'd be taking off in his Jeep with a rushed good-bye.

Life isn't about milestones and accomplishments. It's about being present in others' lives.

Willie ended up beside her while the video played. She wrapped an arm around him and kissed him on the cheek, right above his beard.

"Thank you."

As the video ended with recent pictures and footage of John Luke, everybody clapped and some even wiped tears from their eyes. Korie went over to her eldest son and gave him a big hug.

Yeah, she was crying. But that was okay.

"It's not like I'm leaving for good," John Luke said to everybody. "It's just college. There's

Christmas break, and I might end up coming back to live with you guys when I'm done."

"Hey now," Willie said from across the room. "That's not part of the plan. We talked about this."

He was joking like he usually did.

As Korie wiped her eyes, she caught a glimpse of Hunter sitting in a chair watching her. He forced a sad smile onto his lips, then looked away.

29
FELIZ NAVIDUCK

Hunter lay on the cot playing Candy Crush on his phone and realized it needed charging. He'd tried calling his father an hour ago but only reached his voice mail. He'd sent Carson a text but hadn't gotten one back. He kept waiting and wondering when they'd reply, but his phone remained silent. He plugged it into the charger and tried to ignore it for a while.

It was quiet in John Luke's room. Just like the quiet in Hunter's life. A playlist of silence—not even the same song played over and over again, not even static.

He kept picturing Willie and Korie standing next to John Luke. He couldn't imagine what it would be like having them as his parents. Or even his uncle and aunt. Not because they were famous but simply because they cared. They laughed. They listened.

They love.

For a moment, Hunter looked up at the ceiling.

What would it be like to know someone was there, all the time, always caring, always watching out for you?

Hunter knew Mom loved him, but she was gone too much. She was always busy. His mom had never really been a big part of his life before the divorce, and then she found faith and started trying to find Hunter at the same time. It hurt her when he made it clear he wished he were living with his father. They'd argued over this, and Hunter knew she was right. Dad was selfish. Mom at least *wanted* to be with him.

Except for this Christmas, when she sent me away to West Monroe.

He could feel the frustration moving in like a

fog over a seaside town. He couldn't do anything about it. Over and over again he kept thinking what it would be like to have a big, loving family.

Everything would be different. I'd be different.

There was a reason he liked cranking the music and playing on his iPhone. It shut out these thoughts. It shut them up. It brought in the noise of another life while silencing his own talking shadow.

Soon another sound came. It was the door.

"Hey—are you sleeping?" John Luke asked in a whisper.

"Yes," he said with a smile.

"We have to get going soon." John Luke did a gesture that Hunter remembered Phil Robertson doing—a thumbs-up signal.

Hunter was glad to get out of his thoughts and head over to Phil and Miss Kay's place. For some strange reason, he couldn't wait to see them.

"So, Windy City. I see you're still here in Louisiana. We haven't frightened you off yet?"

Phil Robertson looked just like he had the last time Hunter saw him—dressed in camo pants and a white T-shirt. He wore a camo bandanna around his head, and he still didn't have shoes or socks on.

"Not yet," Hunter responded.

"That's good to hear," Phil said. "We can go out and shoot some squirrels if you'd like a little souvenir to bring home with you."

Hunter wasn't sure if Phil was serious or not. The guy still scared him a bit. If it weren't for all of Phil's Jesus and Bible talk, Hunter would probably be terrified of him.

"I have plenty of souvenirs. But thanks."

They had just arrived at Phil and Miss Kay's house about ten minutes ago. The other family members were already there. They all acted like Hunter was part of them. Most of the guys sat around the television while the women visited and cooked in the kitchen. Miss Kay spotted Hunter and made him join her in the kitchen. Phil was in there too, along with two younger women.

"Want some more cooking tips?" she asked.

She must think I'm really going to make food when I get back home.

"Sure," he said.

Hey, isn't Christmas a time for miracles? Hunter in the kitchen would certainly be one.

Miss Kay showed him several pies that waited on the stove, ready to be baked.

"Instead of turkey and dressing, we're going to be eating those," Miss Kay said.

"Pies? Like apple pies or something?"

"Crawfish pies."

For a second Hunter had to adjust his thinking. He had assumed they were something sweet. But crawfish?

"You're gonna love them," she said in her Southern drawl. "We'll be baking those for about thirty minutes each. But that's later. Right now we're going to make some appetizers."

"We?" Hunter asked.

"Yes. I have my helper back. Missy and Jessica, have y'all met Hunter?"

There were some momentary introductions

made. More people he didn't know. More ladies all dressed up. More smiles. More warmth on his face.

"*We* are gonna make crawfish balls," Miss Kay said. "You, me, and Phil. Are you up for it?"

Hunter gave her a nod. "Sure."

"Okay. We start with that big skillet right there."

She and Phil showed him each step in a natural, slow sort of way. Mom and Dad were always too busy to show him anything. Well, Mom was busy and Dad was gone. That meant he'd never really been shown how to cook anything.

Or build anything. Or budget anything. Or be a grown-up in any capacity.

They heated up olive oil in the skillet, then added onions, celery, bell pepper, parsley, and garlic. Then a dash of salt and pepper. They cooked this for ten minutes.

"Get that crawfish over there," Phil told him.

He added the crawfish to the mix along with several cups of bread crumbs and eggs.

"You're going to make those into little balls," Miss Kay instructed. "Ever made meatballs?"

Hunter shook his head. So Miss Kay showed him what to do.

For twenty minutes, Hunter felt like he was rolling up about two thousand crawfish balls (or maybe just around twenty or thirty). Soon he and Phil were frying a few of them at a time.

"The last thing we do is spread this Cajun seasoning on top of them, just like this," Miss Kay said.

Sure enough, the container read, *Duck Commander Cajun Seasoning*.

They really do have Duck Commander everything.

Hunter imagined accidentally setting something on fire as he fried the crawfish balls—maybe even himself. He'd storm out of the kitchen and through the yard, looking for a nearby river or swamp to douse himself in.

"So how do you feel when you're cooking?" Miss Kay asked him.

He hadn't thought about it.

How do I feel?

The answer surprised even Hunter. "It's weird.

When I'm not thinking about accidentally lighting myself on fire, I feel pretty . . . calm."

Miss Kay laughed. "I've always thought cooking soothes the soul."

With so many things to think about and do and check on and mix together, Hunter would never have guessed that cooking could soothe at all. But since arriving in West Monroe, he had discovered that Miss Kay was usually right about these things.

Hunter watched them all as he ate the best meal of his life. It was easy to stay silent and eat while the rest of them talked.

Phil sat at the head of the table, and before they began eating, he'd thanked God for the food and thanked Jesus for coming into the world. For a second this confused Hunter.

Aren't they the same? Or are they different? God's the Father, right?

The prayer didn't sound like it was addressed to some mystical, far-off, Zen-like god but to someone

Phil had talked to many times. Phil spoke in a respectful tone, but also in a tone that sounded like he really knew whom he was praying to.

During the meal, the conversation shifted between everything from duck hunting (which could be expected) to Sadie's boyfriend (which made Hunter listen more closely) to running out of crawfish balls. At one point Jase Robertson asked Hunter to make some more.

"You know you have to do that if we run out of the crawfish balls?" Jase asked. He sometimes seemed more serious than the other brothers, and it was hard to tell when he was joking.

Hunter looked at Miss Kay, who just shook her head. "He's kidding."

There were so many family members here that they ate at three different places: the long dining table, another table near the kitchen, and at the island on barstools. For some reason Phil and Miss Kay had seated Hunter with the adults.

"So what do you think of the crawfish pie?" Phil called out to him.

"I didn't think I liked fish until coming here."

"This isn't just any old fish, you know?" Jase said to him.

"We wake up; we kill; then we eat," Phil said in a way that Hunter imagined Moses might've sounded.

This was a great time for Hunter to publicly thank them all for having him here. The spotlight was momentarily on him, so he had a chance to say something . . .

Come on, Hunter. Say thanks. Say it. Say it.

But the moment passed, and Jep started a new conversation. "Did you see the last Cowboys game? How bad they lost?"

His chance was over.

As always, Hunter had been given an opportunity and he'd failed.

Carson would've said thanks and made them all laugh. You just sit there red-faced and stupid.

Hunter wanted to take his inner voice out back and beat it to a pulp.

But you can't. Na-na-na-na-na.

His father liked to talk about "stepping up to the plate." Whether in baseball or in life, you should swing for the fences. But that's not what Hunter did.

He hated being at the plate. And whenever he got close, he stepped right back.

That's who he was, and unfortunately he didn't think he was ever going to change.

Most people don't change. Even if they really, truly want to. It's hard. Everyone needs a little help.

And for some of us, help's not gonna come.

Ho-ho-ho.

Bah humbug.

30
A HOLLY JOLLY ROBERTSON FAMILY CHRISTMAS

Reed Robertson, Jase's oldest son, was the first to open a wacky present. It was a one-month supply of tattoo removal cream. Everyone laughed, knowing it was a gift from Miss Kay. She always teased Reed about his tattoos, and this was her way of continuing the joke.

"Here we go!" Willie said.

Korie noticed Hunter's confused look as the group sat in the best circle they could so everyone could see each other's gifts.

"We have some ongoing jokes," Korie explained. "Courtesy of Miss Kay."

Opening presents at Phil and Miss Kay's house was always a crazy time. Maybe because it was full of family: Phil and Kay plus the four sons and their spouses, along with all the grandchildren and a few great-grandchildren. It wasn't simply a bit madcap. It was borderline mayhem, especially when Miss Kay's presents were on display.

You never quite knew what you might receive from her. And Korie, just like everybody else, looked forward to seeing Miss Kay's gifts the most.

There were reasons why.

First off, Miss Kay sometimes bought these gifts really early in the year. Like February early. She might be shopping and find something and laugh and think it would be just perfect. But by the time Christmas came around, she'd forget why she thought it was so funny in the first place.

She also liked to be ironic with her presents. Sometimes she'd get something for a family member that made little sense to *them*, while the rest of the group got the joke. Like the time she bought a daily devotional of cheery thoughts for Jase. He thanked her and thought this was a bit odd, but oh, well. What Jase didn't understand was he was the *last* person in the room who would have 365 days of cheery thoughts. This made Miss Kay chuckle in her own way. It made others nervously laugh, wondering what she might have for them.

Miss Kay didn't have a mean bone in her body, so any joking she might do was always harmless and came with an abundance of love. Like Willie's crazy bread, her jokes were full of sweet, warm love.

Another notorious joke was her annual gift for Rebecca Robertson. Every year, Miss Kay would give Rebecca some kind of Asian-inspired present. At first this meant something like a year's supply of chopsticks. But then Miss Kay started confusing Rebecca's ethnicity. One time she bought her a set of Japanese knives.

"Mom, she's from Taiwan," Willie had said. "That's different."

Another time Rebecca received a Korean tea set from Miss Kay.

"Mom, do you know where Korea is?" Willie had said. "It's not Taiwan. You know—the Korean War?"

Maybe somewhere else or with someone else this would be offensive, but Rebecca loved it and said it made her feel closer to the family.

This year, Miss Kay's gift had to do with the boutique store Rebecca and Korie had opened. Inside was a wooden duck and a jar of Thousand Island dressing.

"That's in honor of Duck & Dressing." Miss Kay smiled.

"I don't think they would've guessed that," Jase said.

Following all the talk could feel like a choose-your-own-conversation adventure. One minute Alan was teasing Jep about something; the next John Luke was quoting Korie. Mia might make everybody laugh, and then Uncle Si might say something that made no sense.

It was just another evening with the Robertsons.

Korie wondered what Miss Kay was going to give Hunter. He'd already opened a couple of

presents, and each time he had appeared both surprised and embarrassed. But he had thanked everybody and been polite in his responses.

*He's with us. He's here and he's not distracted or
disengaged.*

That's all she'd wanted from the start. To try to
connect with him in some kind of authentic way.
To not force the issue or be sappy about it.

When Hunter picked up his last present, he
did so with a funny grin on his face. It was as if
he too knew who'd given him this gift. He tore the
wrapping paper off the large present. Soon he was
opening the box.

It turned out Hunter didn't receive just one gift
but a whole box of joy from Miss Kay.

The first thing he pulled out was a framed photo.

"Wow," Hunter said. "I've always wanted this."

It was a picture of Oprah. The Chicago connec-
tion, obviously.

The next was some kind of big bowl.

"Thank you," he told Miss Kay.

"That's a really *deep* dish. Get it?"

Everybody laughed, including Hunter. The corny gift really cracked him up.

He pulled out a Chicago Cubs tie. This got the guys talking sports temporarily. Then a replica of the Sears Tower.

"You know this isn't even called the Sears Tower anymore?" Hunter said.

"What? What's it called?" Miss Kay asked.

"The Willis Tower."

"They named it after me," Willie said.

"Not the Willie Tower," Jase said. "They don't want to curse the building. Nobody would live there."

"Is that Willis from *Diff'rent Strokes*?" Alan asked.

Conversation went astray with half the group wondering what in the world *Diff'rent Strokes* was and the other half talking about how awesome that TV show happened to be.

Korie glanced at Hunter with a smirk. "If you don't hurry up, we'll be here till midnight."

The final gifts he lifted from the box were a Chicago skyline snow globe and a fan. Hunter showed them off and thanked Miss Kay but wasn't sure what the fan had to do with anything.

"Oh, come on, Hunter," Willie said. "You gotta get this."

"Don't you see?" Sadie asked.

"*I* even understand the present," Phil said. "And half the time I don't have a clue."

Hunter appeared to be deep in thought. Then realization crossed his face. He held up the snow globe and the fan. "Is this supposed to be . . . to make a windy city?"

Everybody applauded and cheered him on.

Miss Kay nodded and gave him a big smile. "We like to be creative around here," she said.

If there was one picture Korie should have taken of Hunter and the rest of the Robertsons, it would have been at this moment. A skinny, tall kid wearing jeans and a T-shirt that said *The National* with a surprised and amused look on his face. And he was surrounded by a bunch of men and women and boys and girls who truly enjoyed seeing that look of surprise and wonder.

"Never thought I'd get a fan for Christmas," Hunter said.

Korie didn't know if he was trying to be funny or not, but she thought he might be serious.

"But of course you knew you'd be spending Christmas with all of us, right?" Jase asked.

"Next year it'll be the Kardashians," Hunter said.

Perfect timing. Another loud outburst.

"'Tis the season to be jolly."

And jolly they certainly were.

31

GOD REST YE NOT-SO-MERRY, GENTLEMEN

Christmas Day was coming to an end, and still Hunter hadn't heard from his father. He'd spoken with Mom once, but Dad hadn't called back. So before it got too late, he decided he'd try to call again.

"I don't know if you'll get any service," Korie told him. "You can try."

They'd been playing games and eating dessert and laughing and continuing to celebrate Christmas. Hunter had all but forgotten about home. Until there came a point when he thought about it again and it made him sad. You shouldn't *forget* about home on Christmas. Really, you should *be* at home. Or at least hear from those who are back home. Those who supposedly love you.

I'll never understand my father. I'll never figure him out.

But Hunter didn't want to give up. He wanted to tell his father how this trip had been. He didn't want to wait. That's all he ever did when it came to Dad. Wait and wonder.

So Hunter slipped out of the house and went into the chill of the night to try to call one more time. He actually got service—a couple of bars— on his iPhone. So the call went through.

He reached his father.

"Hunter? What are you doing?"

Some Christmas greeting that was.

I'm doing what you should've done eight hours ago.

"I just wanted to call," he said in a weak voice. "Before the day was through."

"You having a good time?"

His father sounded animated. Extra happy. Which

meant he'd probably been having a little too much spiked eggnog. A little too much holiday cheer.

"Yeah," Hunter said. "I just thought I'd call."

"You surviving with all those crazy country folk?"

Hunter felt something strange inside him. He suddenly felt defensive. For the Robertsons, of all people.

"They're not crazy country folk," he said.

"Oh, I know that. I'm just kidding. You surviving? I bet you want to come home."

"No, not really. It's been a pretty amazing time."

"Really? See? You need to listen to me more often."

"Wasn't this Mom's idea?" he reminded his father.

"Wow—you're sounding like you want a fight tonight."

"I just thought it'd be nice to talk."

"You want to talk to Carson? I can see if he's around."

"No, it's fine," Hunter said. *If Carson won't bother to text me back, I don't have to bother to talk to him.*

"So you're coming back tomorrow, right? Your mother's going to be picking you up. Did she tell you that?"

How convenient. Hunter was quiet.

This had not gone as he had planned. He wasn't sure what exactly he'd expected, but it wasn't hearing Dad's slightly drunk voice. His energetic, having-the-time-of-his-life voice. This was the way things used to be, one of the reasons Hunter's parents finally separated. Dad loved having a good time away from his family. Now he was doing the same thing again, except Carson the college student was somewhat a part of his life now.

"You there?" Dad asked.

"Yeah. I gotta go," Hunter said.

"Hey, come on, buddy. Cheer up."

Buddy.

Hunter sighed.

Hey, old buddy, old pal.

Maybe if Hunter were Daniel Clarke's drinking partner, he'd smile and laugh and enjoy some more conversation. But Hunter was the seventeen-year-old son he saw only a handful of times a year.

"Merry Christmas, Dad." He didn't wait to hear the reply.

They always sounded the same.

In the middle of the country, under a stark moon that seemed to gloat over him, Hunter decided to keep walking down the road.

He'd brought something with him in case he needed to feel a little "happy, happy, happy." He wanted to curse everything and slip away for a moment. So that's what he did.

Maybe there was a God above, but if there was, he was paying attention to the house Hunter had just left.

And Hunter didn't blame God for overlooking him.

Everybody else did.

32
HERE WE LEAVE
A-CAROLING

"What if something happened to him?"

Korie sat in the passenger seat while Willie climbed in and started the SUV.

He put a hand on her leg. "It's going to be fine. It's not like Hunter has a car. He probably just went walking down the street."

"But why? Did something go wrong that I missed?"

"What? You don't remember what you said to him that drove him into the cold wilderness to fend for himself?"

"Come on," Korie said.

Willie was still in fun mode, but Korie wasn't joking around. She couldn't imagine something happening to Hunter. What would she say to his mother? To his family?

"Calm down for a moment," Willie said as they drove away from Phil and Kay's house. "Nothing happened to him. Maybe he needed a break from everybody. I get that way like every hour."

"I thought he was having a good time," Korie said.

"He was."

"Then what happened?"

"He said he was going to make a call."

Korie glanced at Willie. "To whom?"

Willie shrugged. "Assuming maybe his family. Or his girlfriend. Or maybe his parole officer who *could* be his girlfriend, too, which would really be ironic if you think about it."

"Stop. This isn't funny."

"That'll be bad if we don't find him. National headlines: the Robertsons invite a child to spend Christmas with them and *lose* him."

"Willie, come on."

There was a stretch where the road edged around the nearby lake. Willie seemed to have an idea because he slowed down at a spot overlooking the water. The lights from the SUV quickly revealed a figure standing at the shore of the lake and holding something between his fingers.

"Is he smoking?" Korie asked.

"Yeah." Willie drove closer and parked the car. "And I have a feeling that's not a cigarette." Willie wasn't joking anymore. "Here. Let me talk to him."

"What are you gonna say?" Korie asked.

"It'll be okay."

"Willie, be nice."

He laughed. "What do you think I'm going to do? Toss him in the water or something? Just let me talk to him, all right? We'll stay down here for a while. I don't want him smelling like pot. Or acting all goofy."

"Are you sure?"

"Yeah," Willie said. "It'll be fine. Head on back to Phil and Kay's. We'll walk. If I need to, I'll drive him home from there and pick y'all up later." They climbed out of the SUV and Korie got behind the wheel.

"Text me if you need something."

"Don't worry," Willie said. "Unless you hear police sirens. Then maybe come find us."

33
NOT-SO-WONDERFUL CHRISTMASTIME

Escape is possible.

Yet Hunter knew the truth about this whole idea of escaping. You had to know where you were going, where you were planning to run. There was little joy in getting away if you didn't have an ultimate destination in mind.

But for seventeen years, Hunter had simply been escaping. Trying to get out of things and situations. Leaving conversations and departing the scene and avoiding the relationship and abandoning the commitment. He'd been a prisoner on the run for so many years, yet he really hadn't escaped *to* anywhere. He still found himself running around with his hands cuffed and his eyes blindfolded.

He had walked here just to get away. Just to have a smoke and depart reality for a while. The irony was that the reality he wanted to escape from wasn't the boredom back home or the empty spaces his parents had left behind.

No.

He had wanted to leave this night because the contrast made him sad. It reminded him of his father and his brother and all the things he was missing out on. And the feelings were like lead weights attached to his ankles, pulling him deeper and deeper underwater.

Then he saw the piercing lights cutting through the dark night. And soon enough, Willie was walking toward him.

Hunter didn't even bother getting rid of his pot.

"Kinda cold to be checking out the lake, don't you think?" Willie said when he walked up to him.

Hunter nodded. He raised the joint to his lips again.

"Whoa, whoa—don't even think about it," Willie said. "Get rid of that."

So Hunter snubbed out the joint and tossed it from his hand. The two of them stood in the darkness.

"Were the Christmas presents *that* bad?" Willie said in a joking tone. "Did we make you take off?"

He shook his head but said nothing.

"Look—I get it. Doesn't mean it's gonna be allowed. But I have friends who still struggle. They're doing stupid stuff. I've done stupid stuff. But do you want to keep doing stupid stuff all your life? Do you want to find yourself thirty, forty, fifty years old still wondering when you're gonna stop being so stupid?"

"Nothing's going to change when I get back home."

Willie nodded. "Then be responsible for the one person you can change—*you*."

"Yeah, but I'm not going to be able to change anything," Hunter said. "People don't change."

Willie laughed. "Says who?"

"You don't know my family."

"Oh, what? Are you *so* different?"

"I can't make anybody change."

"Really. Listen up. You know my father's story, right? He told you he was a wild man. Abandoned his family. Left us. God changed him."

"Yeah, well, miracles happen," Hunter said.

"Oh yeah? You think it's only someone like Phil?"

"Yeah."

"Look, Mr. Windy City. Korie has an uncle named Mac Owen. A great man. Married to an amazing woman named Mary. Wonderful family. There was a time when he almost lost it all. Just like Phil. A meth user out of his mind. And you know who God used to change it all?"

"His wife?"

"No. Yes, but no. Really it ended up being the words his four-year-old daughter told him one day that finally woke him up. God can use anybody, Hunter. *Anybody.* Look at us. Look at our family. People might see us on the streets and think we're homeless, might want to throw a few dollars in our cups. Or they might think we're building a bomb in the middle of the woods based on the way we look. But God's been using us for a while and it's pretty cool."

"I don't have a beard."

"Yeah. But you got a sharp mind. You just have to realize God has a place for you, Hunter. Doesn't matter who you are or where you've been."

Hunter wiped tears from his eyes. They must've come because he was feeling the pot and getting all tingly inside.

"Now let's get back to the house," Willie said. "And I don't want to see that stuff anymore. Not one more time. It's Christmas, okay? It's not Cheech & Chong's Christmas special. Come on."

"I'm sorry."

"Don't apologize to me. Just imagine God up there telling you to 'cut 'em.' How do you think you'd feel? That's what he's doing, but he doesn't say you should go alone. He wants you to trust him before you aim and fire. To trust him *with your life*."

Willie's words rattled around in Hunter's head all the way back to Phil and Kay's.

Hunter didn't say anything as they all drove back to Willie and Korie's house later that night. Before he could head upstairs, Willie took him aside and punched him gently in the shoulder. He seemed to have more to say.

"Think about something, Hunter. What if I said, 'Hey, here you go. Take John Luke. Take him and do whatever you want to him. He's yours. I'm doing this 'cause I love you'?"

"What?"

"Yeah, exactly. *What?* But this whole thing. The tree. Those lights. The presents and everything. It's about that. That gift. That crazy gift to fools like you and me. I still don't get it, but man, do I believe in it and cherish it. The God *of this universe* said, 'Here you go.' And he didn't have a Son to spare. And he gave him to die for us. It's an amazing thing."

Hunter didn't know what to say. He probably couldn't say anything if he tried.

"It's not only an amazing thing," Willie said. "It's enough. Enough to take care of the rest of the world. A simple gift changed the universe for all eternity. So remember that tomorrow when you leave and head home. I have to step back and remember it myself."

Hunter ached all over. He looked out the window toward the shadowy sky. "I wish I could believe like you do."

"You can," Willie said. "You really and truly can."

34
I NEED TO BE AWAY in a MANGER

Christmas was coming to a close. Korie was so tired she felt afraid sleep might not come. Her mind still raced even though her body had thrown in the towel an hour ago. She was cleaning up a bit in the kitchen when Willie came up and gave her a hug.

"Did everything work out with Hunter?" she asked.

Willie grabbed some water out of the fridge. "Yeah. It's all good."

"Are you still okay taking him to the airport tomorrow?"

"Yeah, sure."

"I hate that I won't be able to take him."

"You've done enough," Willie told her.

"Thank you for making John Luke's video."

"Aw—you've thanked me enough. It was fine."

"It was more than fine. It was awesome. It means a lot."

"Hey, maybe he will end up living with us another ten years," Willie joked.

They laughed.

"Worse things could happen," she said.

"Stop cleaning—you need to get to bed."

"I will," Korie said. "Just give me a few minutes."

Willie left her alone in the kitchen. She saw presents scattered on the dining room table and on the island in the kitchen. They were so blessed. It had been a good day.

Once again she thought of the video and of the coming days when, one by one, the children would forge lives for themselves. When doors would open and they would race through them without looking back. Willie and Korie wanted them to, expected them to run the race. But that didn't mean she didn't feel a little fear when the door shut behind them.

It still seemed like it wasn't that long ago when Willie finally asked her to marry him. When she said yes and surprised her parents. When they were just starting out with everything. Careers. A family. Making it day by day.

Blink. Then boom. It's like we're in some kind of crazy time machine.

Korie began to shut off the lights, then noticed the framed Bible verse on the wall. It was one of her favorites.

> *Teach us to number our days,*
> *that we may gain a heart of wisdom.*
> PSALM 90:12

Each passing day, this verse meant a little more to her.

For parents, the days are long but the years are short. The exhausting, exasperating moments are eclipsed by the eternally important ones.

The bundle in her arms became a tiny hand searching for Mommy's. The young kid pedaling away became a figure behind the steering wheel. Those precious little eyes looking up at her were soon facing her with a shadow of yesterday.

There were many things Korie had wanted to do in her life, but being a mother had always been at the top. And this challenging, crazy, chaotic choice had never stopped creating joy in her heart and soul.

So many memories filled her thoughts, yet she refused to let them darken the sky above her.

The best can still be yet to come. The best can still be tomorrow. And the next.

Korie refused to live in the past and resisted letting the future overshadow anything. Whenever this happened, she felt like she was in the middle of a tug-of-war that couldn't be won. She would continue to do what she always did. To simply love those around her and clutch thankfulness in both hands.

Grateful for the gifts surrounding her, laughing alongside her, living and breathing around her.

Thank you, God, for another Christmas. And for a reason to celebrate it.

It was time to get some sleep. Tomorrow was coming.

She couldn't wait to find out what it would bring.

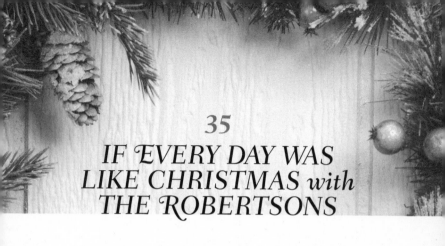

35

IF EVERY DAY WAS LIKE CHRISTMAS with THE ROBERTSONS

The good-byes at the Robertson house had been short and sweet. Rebecca wasn't around when Hunter left—she had to be at her store early. Will simply offered a fist bump. Bella shook his hand, and Sadie hugged him. John Luke, who was carrying his suitcase, walked out with him to the car and gave him a handshake.

"Thanks for staying with us," John Luke said.

Even now, Hunter had to shake his head. "Yeah, you're very welcome," Hunter joked. "It was such a hard thing to do."

John Luke laughed.

Korie gave him a big hug. "I'm sorry I can't ride with y'all. I have to be at a meeting this morning."

"It's fine."

This is your opportunity to say thanks—to say something, anything. *Don't blow it, Hunter.*

"Thank you for everything," he said.

"You're certainly welcome."

Say more. Say what you really feel—say it all; get it out.

"Tell your mother thank you," Korie told him.

He nodded. "I had a good time."

"We did too."

But there's more. It was more than just a good time. It was unbelievably more.

"Here's one more little present," Korie said, giving him a small box. "Open it on the plane."

"Okay." Then he climbed into the SUV.

Sometimes the things that needed to be said took time to figure out. Sometimes simple words didn't truly sum them up.

Sometimes you just had to wait.

Soon Hunter found himself leaving the driveway and the neighborhood as Willie drove toward the airport.

After riding in silence for a few minutes, Hunter told Willie the truth. How he was really feeling.

"I don't want to go back home."

Willie paused for a moment and looked at him. "Your family is waiting on you."

"Yeah, and it's kind of awful knowing that, especially when you think that there are families like yours out there."

"Son . . . this family of ours—we're not perfect or anything."

"You're pretty close to it."

"No. Hunter, look at me. No, we're not. We're just incredibly blessed. I wasn't the cause of it. Korie didn't do this. Phil didn't. Nobody did. Nobody here on this earth. We owe this to God."

"See—even there you say the right thing."

Willie chuckled. "I'm not tryin' to say any 'right' or 'noble' thing. It's the truth as I see it."

"My truth is an empty house. Divorced parents.

An older brother who doesn't even know me. Or care about me. A father I'm beginning to despise."

There was a pause.

"Does he ever physically hurt you?" Willie asked.

"No. It's worse than that."

"What?"

"He ignores me."

Willie stared out the window for a moment as they pulled up to the curb at the airport. "You know—this is what I believe. What I've been taught and what I feel deep down. There's a place where the house is never empty. A place that's never silent. A home where baggage isn't carried in or out. A place where we're light and free and where we're finally the people God meant us to be."

"Can you give me that address?" Hunter asked.

"No," Willie said. "But I can tell you how to get there. In fact, we gave you an instruction manual with your name printed on the cover."

Hunter laughed and looked out his window, away from Willie, trying to hide his tears. He attempted to casually wipe his eyes, but nothing about this was casual.

This was one of those moments you remember. For a really long time. He wasn't that old but he was old enough to understand the importance of this conversation.

"I like the sound of that," Hunter said, still not looking at Willie.

"What's that?"

"Being light. Being free."

"Yeah. I can't wait."

And that was it.

Those were the words that somehow did the most damage. Those four words sank in the deepest.

"Yeah." A simple agreement from Willie. *"I can't wait."*

Acting like he was in the same boat. Sounding like he was weighted down just like Hunter.

Really?

Willie had said it in a simple, straightforward manner.

Hunter finally met Willie's eyes. "Thank you," he said, feeling his heart racing and his face getting flushed. "Thank you for letting me spend Christmas with you."

"Of course."

"Please thank Mrs. Robertson again."

"I will."

"Tell her I'm sorry for wandering off and smoking. And for my attitude. Just tell her that."

Willie nodded. "Listen, I've had to apologize to Korie more than you'd believe. She accepts apologies. She gives grace freely and without questions."

There were so many words filling Hunter inside. Yet he couldn't find a net to scoop them up and spill them out.

"Please let her know I'm thankful."

"I will. And, Hunter, I'm not going to say anything about your parents, okay? But listen—you're a good guy. You're smart and funny and people like you. Well, when you don't have a bad attitude they do. But don't view yourself the way you think others might. Okay? Remember: the God of this universe loves you the same way he loves all his children. With the same amount of love. There are no favorites in God's Kingdom. And I'm so, so thankful for that."

Hunter nodded but didn't say anything.

"Now you better go or you'll miss your plane," Willie said.

"That might be a good thing."

"Your folks wouldn't like it," Willie said. "Well, I know your mother wouldn't."

Hunter gave him a smile and opened the door. Willie followed and pulled out his suitcase.

"Bring a little of West Monroe back to Chi-town, okay?" Willie said.

"I'll do my best."

Willie extended his hand and Hunter accepted it. Then he walked through the sliding-glass doors and toward the counter.

When he finally got through security and headed for his gate, Hunter saw a Duck Commander sign in one of the gift shops. At the center were large photos of Phil and Willie. Hunter could only laugh.

He knew he hadn't come to West Monroe by accident.

God had a forever family in mind for Hunter. And he also had a great sense of humor.

But most of all, God loved Hunter.

He was starting to really believe that.

36

HAVE YOURSELF A HOPEFUL LITTLE CHRISTMAS

Hunter opened the box from Korie on the plane. He was already feeling strange for getting all teary-eyed thinking about leaving West Monroe. Thinking about maybe never seeing the Robertsons again in his life. He might have met real, genuine people before now, but he'd never met the kind who got his spirit and his soul beating. Who got the songs in his heart playing again. Who turned on his inspiration with a button that had long been forgotten.

The first thing in the box was a letter. Something else was underneath it, wrapped in paper. He unwrapped this and saw an ordinary-looking duck call.

So I finally got my duck call.

He unfolded the letter and saw a woman's handwriting.

Dear Hunter,

You're probably wondering why, of all the things I could have given you, I chose a duck call. It's not even personally engraved or anything.

But I'll tell you a secret. It's actually one of the first official Duck Commander calls ever made. It's from Phil's original batch, years ago. To be honest, it might be worth something. I'm not sure.

I hope you're wondering why I gave it to you. I really do.

Two important things happened in Phil Robertson's life. For him and for the rest of the family. The first was that he turned his life over to Jesus after spending more than ten years running away from him. Then he decided to try making an amazing duck call and realized he could. He had a vision.

Nobody expected this guy who had failed and messed up his whole life to do anything. But Miss Kay stood behind him and his family supported him.

You know what, Hunter?

It's amazing.

Amazing what someone can do with a dream and the faith and fire to pursue it.

I was already a part of the family when the seeds were first being sown. When the beards were barely there. When nobody had ever heard of Phil Robertson and his duck calls.

All you can do is work hard and pray. God doesn't promise us an easy life. He does promise blessings, but we can't always imagine what they will be.

You are young and you have your whole life ahead of you. I know you're a talented kid, and I know you have a good heart.

Know that God has a plan for you. He does. And he really, truly wants the best for you. You just have to love him and realize your purpose here isn't for yourself. You have a reason for being you, Hunter. You really do.

Thanks for spending Christmas with our family. We hope some of the moments were fun and memorable. You'll always have a place here with the Robertsons. Remember that. We're busy, but we also want to always—always— have an open door.

Christmas is about celebrating gifts, and you were the gift God gave us this year. I hope you truly realize that.

Have a safe trip back home. And know that you'll always be welcome here—the cot is yours whenever you want to come visit.

Korie and the rest of the Robertsons

For a long moment—maybe the longest moment in Hunter's life—he just sat there looking at this letter. Wondering if it was real. Trying to understand the words written there. Rereading them to make sure he'd really read them. Then looking at the duck call.

It felt strange to be spoken about like this. To be highlighted. To be considered at all.

For the last few days, he'd been angry wondering why his own family couldn't be more like what he needed, angry that he had to go back to his old life. But now he didn't feel that way.

Now he found himself happy and quite a bit humbled that this family had given him their time. They'd let him in. And they'd noticed him. To them, he was not just a random kid but a real person who was somebody.

It was pretty cool. Pretty surreal.

And he had one person to thank for this. His mother.

Well, maybe two, actually.

He saw Mom waiting by the car. A woman he barely recognized because he'd never bothered to look her way and really study her.

Hunter suddenly realized there was probably no way to know the extent of his mother's love for him.

But the last few days had all been because of an incredible gift she gave him.

That God gave me.

"Hey, Hunter, how are you—?"

Hunter didn't let her finish the greeting. He hugged his mother in a way he couldn't ever remember hugging her before. Maybe when he was a toddler and when the notion of hanging on to your mother was just a given. But now he held her to try to let her know how much he appreciated her.

"Thank you," he finally said.

"For what?"

"For thinking I might need to go down to West Monroe."

"Did you have a good time?" Mom looked surprised and thrilled.

"Yeah, you could say that."

"I'm glad, Hunter. I didn't know—I wasn't sure. Even when I thought it might be a miracle, I didn't know if it was the right thing sending you down there."

"It was the perfect thing. It was awesome."

"Did you meet some great people?"

"Yeah. They're some kind of people."

"Really?" Mom asked. "They weren't too crazy?"

"Just enough to think I was something special."

In the car, he told his mother something that had been on his mind for a while.

"Can you do me a favor before we get home?" he asked.

"What's that?"

"Can you stop by the grocery store?"

"Well, I already have a fully stocked house."

He shook his head. "No. I need to pick up a few things."

"Like what?"

"Like one of your Christmas presents. I'm going to attempt the impossible."

Mom looked at him with a faint smile on her lips. "The impossible?"

"I'm going to cook for you. Or at least try."

It might end in disaster, but it was a start.

Just a start.

EPILOGUE

Maybe it was too much to ask for a Christmas miracle. Coming back home to see his mother and father standing there hand in hand, his brother beside them. The Christmas tree lit and the ham cooking and holiday songs playing in the background.

"The God of this universe said, 'Here you go.' And he didn't have a Son to spare. And he gave him to die for us. It's an amazing thing."

Hunter could hear Willie's words.

"It's enough. Enough to take care of the rest of the world. A simple gift changed the universe for all eternity."

Eternity seemed like such a long time. Some

days simply felt long enough. The hours spent in his lonely home, surrounded by the shadows of memories that hurt to think about.

It's enough.

And maybe it would be.

The silence and the memories awaited. But he was armed now and ready. Prepared to blast out the darkness and the stillness. Planning to open some doors or kick them down if he had to.

Hunter sat in the car outside the suburban house and waited for a moment, feeling his heart beating. How could he be so nervous to go in and see his father and brother? But somehow that's how he felt.

His fist was tightened and he liked the feeling. He opened it and saw the duck call.

Then he remembered what Korie had said in her letter: *"Amazing what someone can do with a dream and the faith and fire to pursue it."*

The dream wasn't to have his family suddenly become the Robertsons. That was impossible. But he did dream of trying to be a part of his father's and brother's lives again. He shouldn't be the one trying, but he was okay with doing so.

"God doesn't promise us an easy life. He does promise blessings, but we can't always imagine what they will be."

Hunter knew he had a long way to go. With giving himself over fully to this whole faith thing. With figuring things out, like his life and what he wanted and where he was going. With his family and how broken they were and how they'd probably never be fully put back together.

But just like this little device in his hand would bring ducks to him, he was going to use this past Christmas as a way to bring Dad and Carson back to him. The only difference was he wasn't going to shoot them down.

He was gonna grab them and never let them go.

And maybe—possibly, hopefully—God was going to do the same with him.

About the Authors

Kay Robertson is the revered matriarch of the Robertson family and star of A&E®'s *Duck Dynasty*®. She was just a teenager when she met and married Phil, and since then she's been keeping him and her boys from spending too much time in the woods by bringing them back to civilization each night with a home-cooked meal. Kay believes her cooking talents are a gift she must share, so she often ends up feeding all of the family and most of the neighborhood.

Critically acclaimed and creatively diverse novelist *Travis Thrasher* has made a career out of defying expectations. Writing stories that have moved, haunted, and provoked readers, Thrasher has told tales in a variety of genres. His one common theme is brokenness, and his one common tactic is surprise. He lives with his wife and three daughters in a suburb of Chicago.